Horrors of the Black Ring

Look for more books in the Goosebumps Series 2000
by R.L. Stine:

Horrors of the Black Ring

AN
APPLE
PAPERBACK

SCHOLASTIC INC.
New York Toronto London Auckland Sydney
Mexico City New Delhi Hong Kong

A PARACHUTE PRESS BOOK

No part of this publication may be reproduced in whole or in part, or stored in a retrieval system, or transmitted in any form or by any means, electronic, mechanical, photocopying, recording, or otherwise, without written permission of the publisher. For information regarding permission, write to Scholastic Inc., Attention: Permissions Department, 555 Broadway, New York, NY 10012.

. ISBN 0-590-68522-8

Copyright © 1999 Parachute Press, Inc.
All rights reserved. Published by Scholastic Inc.
APPLE PAPERBACKS and logo are
trademarks and/or registered trademarks of Scholastic Inc.
GOOSEBUMPS is a registered trademark
of Parachute Press, Inc.

12 11 10 9 8 7 6 5 4 3 2 1   9/9 0 1 2 3 4/0

Printed in the U.S.A.   40

First Scholastic printing, June 1999

"**B**eth — you promised!" my seven-year-old sister, Amanda, whined. "You promised to take me to the petting zoo after school today!"

"I didn't promise you anything," I insisted.

It was a warm spring day. Amanda and I were walking to school.

She buzzed around me like a mosquito. She looks kind of like a bug too. Short black hair, skinny arms and legs like sticks, a pointy little chin, and beady black eyes. I hiked up my baggy cargo pants and swatted her away.

I'm so different from Amanda, you'd never guess we are both in the Welch family. I've got red hair to my shoulders, tons of freckles, round blue eyes, and a round face. I'm not crazy about the way I look. But at least I don't look like an insect.

"Be-e-eth!" Amanda zipped in front of me again. "I *heard* you say it last night. You said, 'Amanda, tomorrow after school I'll do anything you want!'"

I snorted. "I would never say that! Now, get out of my way. You're going to make us late for school!"

"Please?" she begged. "I really miss those cute little goats."

"You don't miss the goats," I shot back. "You miss shooting rubber bands at them."

It's true. She shoots rubber bands at the petting zoo animals. She likes to see how they react. I can't stand it. I love animals. I hate to see them get hurt.

"Besides," I added, "I don't have time today. I've got to work on the Spring Carnival after school."

"Oooo — the Spring Carnival," Amanda teased. "You mean the 'I Love Danny Jacobs Fair'?"

My face suddenly felt hot. "What are you talking about?"

"I know you have a crush on him," Amanda said.

"On Danny Jacobs? You must be crazy!" I shrieked. My voice was just a little too loud.

"You're only working on the carnival because he's the head of it," Amanda accused.

"*I'm* one of the heads too," I reminded her. "We're cochairpeople with Tina Crowley."

"Whatever." Amanda rolled her eyes. "The important thing is, you want to be with Danny. That's why you won't take me to the petting zoo!"

2

"Amanda — shush!" I cried. "You're totally making this up. I —"

I stopped as a shrill scream ripped through the air. I whirled around.

"Anthony — no!" I gasped.

Anthony Paul Gonzales came roaring down the street on his bike.

"Look out!" he shrieked. "No brakes!"

A truck rumbled toward him.

He screamed and swerved onto the sidewalk.

The truck zoomed past. Anthony flew right at us.

"Watch out!" he warned.

At the last second, Anthony squeezed his brakes — and veered away.

Amanda and I clutched each other, trying to catch our breath.

"You jerk! You almost ran us over!" I gasped.

Anthony let out an evil laugh. I hate that laugh.

"Beth, how can you fall for that old 'no brakes' gag?" he asked, grinning. "You're too easy to trick."

"I am not!" I fumed. "You just missed us!"

"You probably didn't even see us," Amanda sneered. "Your sunglasses are too dark."

Anthony proudly adjusted his dark glasses. "Like 'em? My brother gave them to me. They cost a hundred dollars."

"Your brother wasted his money," Amanda muttered.

Anthony is in my sixth-grade class at school. He's tall and thin with short dark hair. He's always playing mean tricks. Not just on me — on everybody. He thinks he's really funny.

Two years ago he told me that my cat, Benson, had been hit by a car. "I saw him lying in the street!" he said.

I screamed and ran outside to check. I loved Benson.

My cat was sitting calmly in the front yard, licking his fur. He was fine. It was only Anthony's idea of a joke.

Benson died of old age last year. When I told Anthony, he laughed. He's totally cold.

Lately, Anthony had been meaner to me than ever. He wanted to be one of the heads of the carnival. But the class didn't vote for him.

He's been playing tricks on me ever since.

I'll get even with him somehow, I thought angrily.

The trouble is, I'm not the get-even type.

I mean, I'm not good at thinking up nasty tricks. Maybe I should take lessons from Amanda. She's great at it.

"See you at school, fool," Anthony sneered. He started to pedal away down the sidewalk.

I noticed something lying on the sidewalk a few feet ahead of him. It was small and black. It twitched.

It's a bird! I realized. And Anthony was about to run over it!

"Anthony, stop!" I screamed.

He didn't stop. He didn't even turn around.

I dove forward and grabbed the seat of his bike. I yanked on it.

He jolted to a stop. "Hey! What's your problem?" he snapped.

I'd stopped him just in time. Anthony had nearly crushed the bird.

"Look!" I cried. "Its wing is broken. And you almost killed it!"

"It's half-dead anyway," Anthony groaned.

I crouched down beside the bird. It struggled to stand up and fly away. But its left wing wouldn't move.

"Poor little birdie," I crooned.

Amanda mimicked me. "'Poor little birdie.' You're such a sap, Beth."

I didn't listen to her. I gently picked up the bird.

"What a goody-goody," Anthony muttered.

"Tell Miss Gold I'm going to be late," I told Anthony. "I'm going to take this little bird home. We'll get him all fixed up. Won't we, little bird?" I stroked the bird's head with my pinkie finger.

"Oh, brother." Amanda sighed. "You really are a goody-goody, Beth."

"Just shut up and go to school," I snapped.

"Hey, Beth — look!" Anthony's dark glasses

5

made him appear even meaner than usual. "You know what bikes are good for? Squishing things!" He pointed at a worm squirming on the sidewalk. Before I could stop him, he rolled his front tire over it.

SQUISH.

"Anthony!" I shrieked. "How could you do that?"

Anthony and Amanda laughed their heads off. "You're so lame," Amanda said.

"I am not!" I cried. "Every living creature is important — even worms! You guys are horrible."

My little speech made them laugh even harder.

"Someday you won't think it's so funny," I warned. "Someday someone will try to squash *you*. Maybe it'll even be me."

Anthony doubled over with laughter.

"I'm so scared," Amanda said sarcastically.

I wheeled around and took the bird home. I had to admit, I could see why they were laughing. Maybe I am kind of a goody-goody. But I don't care.

"I'm sorry I'm late, Miss Gold." I walked into school about an hour later.

Miss Gold smiled at me. "Anthony told me why you were late. How's the sick bird?"

"I think he's going to be okay," I reported. "My mother is taking him to the vet this afternoon."

"Good. That was very responsible of you, Beth." She smiled at me as I sat down in my seat. Her smile is really beautiful. Her teeth are white and perfect and her eyes twinkle.

"Some things are more important than being on time for school," she went on. "Saving a life is one of them. Even if it's only a bird's life."

I beamed as I sat in my seat. Everybody loves Miss Gold.

She looks just like her name sounds. She's young and pretty. Her shiny golden hair comes down to just under her chin. She's even got some freckles sprinkled across her nose. They make her look as if she's still a kid, almost.

"I'm returning your short stories now," Miss Gold announced. "I'm very proud of all of you. This week's stories were excellent!"

Miss Gold began to hand back our papers. When she passed mine to me, I noticed something flash on her hand.

"What's that?" I asked, staring at her finger. "Is that a new ring?"

"Why, yes," she replied. "Do you like it?" She held her hand in front of me so I could see the ring.

It was the strangest ring I ever saw. All black. A large, shiny black jewel was set in a thick black band.

I stared at the jewel. It flashed in my eyes at first, so that I couldn't see it clearly. I grabbed Miss Gold's hand and brought it closer.

I gasped. "Miss Gold — something moved in there. Something is alive inside that ring!"

I stared deep into the ring. A cloudy form shifted inside the jewel. It moved as if — as if it were *alive*.

Miss Gold turned the ring in the light. The cloud became a face. It frowned inside the jewel.

I shuddered. It can't be a face! I thought. It looks so — so evil!

"What *is* that?" I gasped.

"It's a flaw in the jewel," Miss Gold explained. "A cloudy spot. And if you catch it in the right light, it looks like a face, doesn't it?"

I nodded. I couldn't take my eyes off the ring. The face inside it was so ugly. So creepy.

"Such a strange optical illusion," Miss Gold said, almost to herself. "Do you like it?"

I gulped. "Um, I guess so. I can't stop staring at it."

She smiled. "I know. I have the same problem."

"Where did you get the ring?" I asked.

"I found it in the school parking lot," she replied. "I thought I'd wear it until someone claims it."

"Has anyone claimed it yet?" I asked.

"No," she said. "And it's a good thing. Because the ring is stuck on my finger. I-I can't get it off."

She tugged on the ring, showing me. It stuck at her knuckle. "It's almost as if it shrank on my finger," she explained.

Miss Gold passed out the rest of the papers. My eyes kept going back to her ring.

She returned to the front of the room. "I know you're all getting ready for the Spring Carnival," she said. "You've got projects to make for the art sale. And the food committee has a lot of cooking to do. So" — she paused and grinned at us — "I'm not giving you any homework this weekend!"

We all cheered. Miss Gold is the greatest.

We settled down to study geography. Miss Gold pulled a map over to the chalkboard.

Her black ring flashed in the light. I kept thinking about the face in the jewel.

Sure, I thought, it's just some kind of smoky flaw. It only *looks* like a face.

It only *seems* to be moving.

So why is it so creepy?

Why can't I stop thinking about it?

"How could I be so stupid?" I grumbled. I tossed my paintbrush onto the table. I was trying to paint two hands clasped together — a symbol of brotherhood. But I forgot how hard it is to paint hands.

"I ask myself the same question every day," Anthony said. "'How could Beth be so stupid?'"

I glared at him but didn't say anything. He's so mean. And no matter what I say to him, he always gets the last word.

We were in the art room, working on our projects for the carnival art sale. I was in charge of the art sale. Danny was working on games and activities. Tina Crowley was organizing the food.

Everyone in the sixth grade was making something for the sale. I stared at my painting of lumpy, stumpy fingers and sighed. Nobody would want to buy *this* picture.

Anthony peeked over my shoulder. "That's great, Beth," he said. "What's it supposed to be? Why are those worms crawling over that sandwich?"

I could feel my face turning red. I glanced across the room at Danny Jacobs, to see if he'd heard. He was busy molding something out of clay.

Danny is so cute. He's got honey-brown hair, big brown eyes, and really long eyelashes. He's a little taller than I am, and very athletic. He's one of the best players on the soccer team.

"Or maybe you painted two *plants* shaking hands?" Anthony teased.

"If you're so great, let's see what *you're* painting," I replied.

He flashed me a mean grin. "You're going to love it!" he promised.

I stepped up to his easel and gasped. He was painting a round-faced girl with red hair and bulging, crossed eyes.

"Is that supposed to be me?" I cried.

"Ding ding ding! We have a winner!" he crowed. "You guessed right!"

I swallowed. The picture was really ugly. But I didn't want to let Anthony know it hurt me.

"I don't look like that," I sniffed. "Maybe if you took off your sunglasses you'd see me better."

11

Anthony tugged the dark glasses down his nose and stared at me. "Nope — sorry," he said. "I can see better with my sunglasses on. It must be the glare bouncing off your pasty skin."

I opened my mouth to say something back — something good and mean. But the meanest thing I could think of was "Oh, yeah?"

I closed my mouth.

Someday I'll get him good, I fumed. If I could only think of a way . . .

I decided to ignore him. I had no other choice. I glanced across the room at Danny. He was washing the clay off his hands.

Maybe this is my chance to talk to him, I thought. I crossed the room and stood beside him at the sink.

"Hi," I said.

He dried his hands. "Hi. How's your art project going?"

"Not so great," I admitted. I cleared my throat. "Um — do you think you could help me with something? I'm trying to paint hands, and I can't get the fingers right. Could I use your hands as a model?"

Danny nodded. "Sure. I'm waiting for my clay pot to dry, anyway."

He came over to the table and set his hands flat. "Like this?" he asked.

"That's good," I replied. I picked up my brush and started fixing up the worm fingers. I could feel

Danny watching. It made me nervous. I had a hard time concentrating with him sitting right there.

What if he thinks my picture is lame? I thought.

"Oo, look at the lovebirds!" Anthony poked his head around his easel. He made juicy kissing noises. *SMACK, SMACK, SLUUURP.*

Oh, no, I thought. I should have known this would happen.

"Shut up, Gonzales," Danny snapped at him.

Nothing could make Anthony stop. "Beth is painting her true love. Can I come to the wedding?"

"Anthony — stop it!" I cried. He's ruining everything, I thought. Just as he always does.

Anthony puckered up and made the kissy sounds again.

Danny leaped to his feet. "You're looking for major trouble."

"Hey — watch out. I know karate!" Anthony shot back.

Danny threw himself at Anthony and knocked him to the floor. Anthony's sunglasses flew across the room.

"Danny — don't!" I pleaded.

They rolled around on the floor, kicking and punching and crashing into chairs.

"Hey, hey, HEY!" Mr. Martin, the art teacher, raced over to pull the boys apart. "What's going on here? Have you lost your minds?"

Anthony leaped up, wiping his nose. "He jumped me. For no reason at all. He's crazy! He just attacked me!"

"Not true!" Danny protested. "He asked for it."

"All right, all right." Mr. Martin sighed. "Danny, go back over there where you were working before. Anthony, you stay here. Stay away from each other. And if I catch you fighting again, you're both going to the principal's office."

Danny frowned and went back to the clay table. Anthony leaned close to me and whispered, "Wave bye-bye to your boyfriend!"

"Anthony, you stink!" I muttered.

"Ouch! That hurt!" he teased.

I can't stand him.

He went back to the easel. He started painting very quickly, humming as he worked.

I knew he was adding to the ugly picture of me. I had to see what he was painting. I couldn't help myself.

I glanced at his paper. He was painting snot-colored drips running out of my nose.

"Like it?" he asked. "I was thinking of giving it to Danny. I know he'll want a picture of his girl-friend to hang inside his locker."

I hate him. I really hate him. Did I mention that?

After art class, Danny caught up with me in the hall. I was on my way to the cafeteria for lunch.

"Anthony is a total pain," Danny said. "He's always in my face."

"Mine too," I replied. I smiled. Maybe Anthony did me a favor after all. His bad jokes were bringing Danny and me together!

"Can I sit with you at lunch?" Danny asked me. "I'd like to tell you about some ideas I have for the carnival."

Yes! I thought. A little shiver of excitement shot through my skin. Stay cool, I told myself. Don't act too goofy.

"Sure," I said, trying to sound as if it was no big deal to sit next to the cutest boy in the class. "You know —"

A shrill scream interrupted me.

"Huh? What was that?" I gasped.

"It came from in there." Danny pointed to Miss Gold's room. We turned and burst into the classroom as another scream ripped through the air.

Miss Gold stood by the chalkboard, her face twisted in horror.

"What happened?" I cried. "What's wrong?"

Trembling, the teacher pointed to the chalkboard.

Every inch of it was covered with words. Someone had scrawled them over and over: THE CARNIVAL IS DOOMED. THE CARNIVAL IS DOOMED. THE CARNIVAL IS DOOMED.

"Wow," Danny gasped. "This is sick."

"Who did it?" I demanded.

Miss Gold's face crumpled, as if she were about to burst into tears. "I don't know!" she wailed. "I only left the room for a few minutes!"

Wow, I thought. Miss Gold is really upset.

I stared at the scribbled words. "Who would do this?"

"It's got to be a joke," Miss Gold murmured.

"What if it isn't a joke?" I asked. "What if somebody is serious about this?" Danny glanced at me. "What if someone is planning to do something horrible? Really horrible?"

Miss Gold shook her head. She didn't seem so upset anymore. "I don't think so. I'll bet someone is just trying to scare us a little."

"Well, anyway, we'll erase the chalkboard," I offered.

"Yeah," Danny agreed. "No problem."

"Thank you." Miss Gold sighed. "That's sweet of you guys."

I grabbed an eraser and tossed another one to Danny. We started to work, erasing the scrawled words.

The carnival is doomed. The carnival is doomed.

The words repeated in my head, over and over. What did they mean?

Everybody loves the spring carnival, I thought. Why would anyone want to ruin it?

"Hey, guys, what's the word?" Anthony strolled into the room. "Playing teacher's pet again, Beth?"

"Somebody scribbled all over the chalkboard," Danny told him. "Want to help us?"

"Hey — I'd love to, but I can't." Anthony started to back out of the room. "I've got bad allergies, you know. Chalk dust makes me sneeze."

I stepped toward him, waving the chalky eraser. "Oh, yeah? Let's see."

Anthony held up his hands. "Really," he insisted. "I'm serious."

I stared at Anthony's hands.

Hey, wait, I thought.

Anthony's hands — they were covered with chalk dust.

5

"W-what are you looking at?" Anthony stammered, swinging his hands behind his back.

"Your hands are covered with chalk!" I accused.

Danny, Miss Gold, and I stared hard at him. He backed away.

"They — they are not!" he cried. "It isn't chalk — it's clay! I was helping Mr. Martin clean up after art class!"

"Yeah. Sure," Danny muttered. We both knew that helping teachers clean up is *not* the kind of thing Anthony Gonzales usually does.

"I've got to go," Anthony said. He hurried out of the room.

"He's got to go wash the evidence off his hands," Danny said.

"I'll bet Anthony did this," I replied. "He

19

wanted to be in charge of the carnival. But no one wanted him."

"Yeah, I bet he's jealous," Danny agreed.

Miss Gold shook her head. "I can't believe Anthony would do this," she murmured. "The kids in this school are so nice. Nothing like this has ever happened here. . . ."

But it *did* happen, I thought.

Somebody in this school is not so nice. . . .

Amanda started driving me crazy as soon as I got up the next morning.

"Help me arrange my Barbies today!" she begged. "I want to line them all up in order — from prettiest to ugliest."

I sighed. "Amanda, all Barbies look exactly the same. One can't be prettier than another."

"That's not true! Surfer Barbie is beautiful, but Rollerblade Barbie is not so hot."

"Oh, please. Can't you do it yourself? I'm busy. I have to go to school today."

"Liar!" Amanda cried. "It's Saturday!"

"I know that," I replied. "I have carnival stuff to do."

Some of the kids hadn't finished their art projects for the carnival — including me. Also, I was in charge of the art sale, so I had to be there to help.

"But you promised!" Amanda cried.

"I did not!" I insisted. "You're such a liar."

"You're the liar!" she accused. "You never keep your promises, Beth Breath."

"That's because I never make them in the first place — Amanda Panda."

I hate it when she calls me Beth Breath. It sounds like I have bad breath or something — and I don't. And Amanda Panda just doesn't sound as bad.

"That stupid carnival takes up all your time. What about my cow eyeball?"

"Cow eyeball? What are you talking about?" I told you she was nuts.

"For my science class. The teacher said we could make up our own project. So I decided to dissect a cow eyeball. To see what's inside. And you said you'd help me!"

"Yuck. Where on earth did you get a cow eyeball?" I asked.

"I've had it in my room for a week. I got it from Teddy Jackson." Teddy Jackson is a boy in her class. His father works in some kind of lab. Teddy is always giving Amanda gross stuff to keep in her room.

"I can't believe you brought a real cow eyeball into the house," I said. "And you think *I'm* going to cut into it with a knife? You're crazier than I thought."

"You're crazy for liking Danny Jacobs!" she shot back.

"I don't like him!" I protested. "I'm sorry, Amanda, but I can't help you today. Maybe after the carnival is over."

"That will be too late!" Amanda started throwing one of her world-famous temper tantrums. "My project is due Monday!"

"I said I was sorry. There's nothing I can do about it."

"You'll be sorry, all right!" Amanda screeched. "Just wait and see!"

She slammed the door.

I hurried to the kitchen to find Mom. She always hides out in the kitchen when she hears me fighting with Amanda.

"Everything okay?" she asked when I stormed in.

"Why did you have to have another baby after me?" I demanded. "I would have been so happy as an only child."

Mom just shook her head. "Someday you'll be glad to have a sister."

I didn't think that day would ever come. But I kept my mouth shut. I had something else on my mind.

"Where's the bird?" I asked. "Did you take him to the vet?"

Mom nodded. "The vet put a splint on its wing. I bought a little cage for it on my way home. It's out on the back porch."

I went out to the porch. The little bird sat quietly in the cage. Mom had left him a pile of birdseed. It didn't look as if he'd eaten much of it.

"How are you, little bird?" I cooed. "How's your broken wing?"

His wing was bandaged and it looked heavy. Poor little guy, I thought. He doesn't look too good.

I decided to name him Chirpy. I knew it was a stupid name. But I couldn't think of anything better.

I sat outside on the porch for a while. I thought it would be nice to keep Chirpy company.

After a while, Mom called me in to lunch. "How's the bird doing, honey?" she asked.

"Not so great," I answered.

"Maybe he'll be better tomorrow," Mom said. "Amanda, did you see Beth's bird?"

"She should have let Anthony run over it," Amanda muttered.

"How can you be so mean?" I demanded. "You and your cow eyeballs."

"I'm not speaking to you, Beth Breath," Amanda said.

"Good," I replied. "I don't want to hear anything you have to say, anyway."

"Girls —" Mom pleaded.

The rest of the lunch was pretty quiet. We talked to Mom. But we wouldn't talk to each other.

"I wish your father was here," Mom grumbled. Dad was away on a business trip. "Every time he goes out of town, you girls start fighting."

After lunch I hurried to my room. I had to get ready to go to school.

As I grabbed my sweater, the phone rang. I have a phone in my room with my own separate line.

I picked it up. "Hello?"

"*Stay away,*" a strange voice whispered. The voice was muffled — as if someone were trying to disguise it.

"*Stay away. I'm warning you. Don't go to school today.*"

ello? Who is this?" I demanded.
"Anthony? Is that you?"

CLICK.

The caller hung up.

I sat on my bed, shaking. I couldn't help thinking about what had happened in Miss Gold's room the day before.

The carnival is doomed.

Was that Anthony? I asked myself. Hard to tell. The voice was so muffled. It could have been anybody.

Then I heard a noise from Amanda's room. Giggling.

Oh, no, I thought. Not Amanda! It wasn't Amanda.

I flew out of my room and burst into hers. She

25

lounged on her bed, cradling the cordless phone against one ear.

"Amanda — was that you?" I demanded angrily.

"Do you mind?" she snapped. "I'm on the phone."

"Did you just call me?" I asked again. "Was that you using that stupid voice?"

She sneered at me. "Why would I call you? If I want to talk to you, I'll bang on the wall." Then she spoke into the phone. "Teddy? I'll call you back."

"You weren't really talking to Teddy," I said.

"Yes, I was. What are you doing? Will you help me set up my Barbies now?"

I stared at her. She's insane, I thought.

It had to be Amanda, I decided. She just wanted to get me to stay home and play with her.

"I'm not going to fall for your stupid tricks," I declared.

I tripped over a couple of her Barbies as I stormed out of the room.

Danny lived about halfway between my house and school. I found him waiting for me on his front steps. We'd planned to go to the art room a little early to set things up for the rest of the kids.

"I hope this won't take too long," Danny said. "I wanted to go bike-riding today."

"That's sounds like fun," I agreed. "Maybe we can both go for a ride after we're done."

Danny didn't say anything. Did he hear me? I wondered. Does he want to go bike-riding with me or not?

I decided not to say anything else.

Mr. Greaves, the custodian, stood outside the door to the school, jangling his keys.

"I'm locking up at four-thirty," he warned us. "Make sure to finish up by then."

"No problem," I said.

It felt strange to be in school on Saturday. The halls were so quiet and empty. The classrooms were closed and dark.

Danny and I walked quickly down the halls, our sneakers squeaking on the shiny floor. The art room was on the second floor, at the back of the building.

The door was closed. Through the glass we could see that the room was dark.

"I guess we're the first ones here," I said.

"I hope it isn't locked," Danny replied. "Mr. Martin said he'd be here."

Danny tried the door. It opened.

I switched on the lights.

"No!" I gasped. "No!"

7

I felt dizzy. My knees started to collapse.

"I don't believe it," Danny groaned.

The art room was completely trashed.

Tables and chairs were knocked over. Art projects were ripped from the walls and crumpled up. Paint splattered the walls and the floor. Bits of paper and glass littered the room.

Danny and I waded through the mess.

"Everything is ruined," I cried. "Everything." I had a sick feeling in my stomach. I suddenly felt cold all over.

Mr. Martin burst into the room. "Hey, guys. I —"

He stopped when he saw the mess. "Oh, no," he moaned. "Oh, no . . ."

"We just walked in," Danny murmured.

"Who could have done this?" I asked.

"I have no idea," Mr. Martin replied. "My car wouldn't start. That's why I'm late. I — I don't believe someone from our school would do a thing like this."

I started to pick through the piles of trash. I recognized a bit of paper on the floor. It showed a stubby finger.

"Here's part of my painting." I sighed. "Someone ripped it to pieces."

"Hey — check this out!" Danny called. He pointed to a piece of paper tacked to the bulletin board.

Mr. Martin and I hurried over. On white paper were the words, scrawled in red: THE CARNIVAL IS DOOMED.

Danny and I looked at each other.

I shivered. This is no joke, I realized. Someone is really trying to ruin the carnival.

But why?

"Whoever did this might still be in the building," Danny said. "Maybe we should take a look around."

Mr. Martin put a hand on Danny's shoulder to stop him. "It might be someone dangerous, Danny."

Then, across the room, I saw something.

One painting hadn't been destroyed. One and only one.

"No!" I gasped. "I don't believe it!"

"What is it, Beth?" Danny asked. "What?"

"Th-that picture —" I stammered, pointing at it. "Why is that one still here?"

The one painting left was the one Anthony painted of me.

I stared at the portrait of me. It hadn't been torn up. But something had been added to it.

Someone had painted bright red drops dribbling out of my mouth. Blood?

"Hey — what's up?" Anthony came bursting into the art room.

I glared at him.

"What? What's going on?" he demanded. His mouth dropped as he saw the mess all over the room. "Huh? Wh-who did this?"

"*You* did!" I blurted out.

"No way!" Anthony cried. "I just got here!"

"Then why is *your* painting the only one that hasn't been ripped to shreds?" I demanded.

Anthony shrugged. "How would I know? Maybe someone recognizes great art."

"Not funny," Mr. Martin scolded sternly. "This is very serious. I may have to call the police."

I gasped. The police? In our school?

Other kids arrived. They all uttered cries of shock and disbelief. Even Anthony appeared to be frightened.

He always seems to have an excuse, I thought. First we catch him with chalk dust on his hands. . . . Now this.

Is Anthony trying to destroy the carnival? Or is he telling the truth?

"All right, everybody!" Mr. Martin shouted. "Calm down. Let's get this place cleaned up."

I grabbed a broom and started sweeping. Tina Crowley came over with a garbage bag to help me.

"I heard about what happened in Miss Gold's room," she said. "The chalkboard?"

I nodded.

"Beth — I'm kind of scared," Tina admitted. "I mean, we're in charge of the carnival. What if somebody really wants to stop it? What if somebody goes after one of us?"

I shuddered. I was thinking exactly the same thing.

"I heard about what happened in the art room on Saturday." Miss Gold greeted us sadly Monday morning. She looks tired, I thought. As if she hasn't been sleeping well.

"I know how important the art sale is for the carnival," Miss Gold added. "So I'm sending you all up to the art room. You can spend the morning making new projects."

Everyone cheered.

Miss Gold smiled at me. She knew I was in charge of the art sale.

"Thank you, Miss Gold," I said.

We all trooped off to the art room. I glanced back at Miss Gold.

She sat at her desk, tugging on the ring. She pulled on it, frowning, twisting it on her finger.

And then she brought it close to her face and examined it. Stared at it, her lips moving — as if she were talking to the face in the ring.

"Hey, Beth!" Tina Crowley caught me on the way to my locker after school.

"Danny and I are baking cookies for the carnival in the home ec. lab," she told me. "Will you help? The carnival's only two days away, and we're a little behind."

"Sure," I agreed. I knew Amanda would be waiting for me at home. She'd probably start begging me to play with her Barbies again.

I followed Tina to the home ec. room. I didn't know her that well, but she seemed nice. She was small, with short blond hair. She always wore skirts and frilly tops.

Danny was already in the kitchen, stirring a big

bowl of cookie dough. Mrs. Jenkins, the home ec. teacher, was on her way out the door.

"Hi, girls." She smiled at me and Tina. "I have to make a phone call. I'll be right back."

She hurried away.

Danny waved at us. "Grab a spoon," he said.

I washed my hands and started dropping dough in clumps onto a cookie sheet.

"I'd better preheat the oven," Tina said. She turned the oven knob to 350 degrees.

"It should be hot enough soon," she added.

I filled one cookie sheet and loaded it into the oven. I grabbed a clean cookie sheet and started filling it up.

A few minutes later, I smelled something funny.

"Is something burning?" I asked.

Tina shrugged. "I don't think so. The cookies take fifteen minutes to bake."

The sharp aroma burned my nose.

"I smell smoke!" Danny cried.

I turned — and saw thick black smoke pouring out of the oven.

"Oh, no!" I cried. I grabbed a pot holder and threw open the oven door.

The oven burst into flames.

Fire roared out of it.

I screamed and covered my face.

"Help!" I shrieked. "Oh . . . help!"

I froze.

I couldn't believe this was happening.

Tina moved fast. She grabbed me and dragged me out of the kitchen.

"Danny, come on!" I cried.

We raced down the hall. I found a red fire alarm and tugged on the lever. A shrieking bell rang through the school.

Then I saw someone running ahead of us.

Anthony.

What's he doing here? I wondered. School is out. Why isn't he home?

We ran outside and stood in the school yard. A few minutes later, fire trucks squealed to a stop. Firefighters hurried inside the building.

Some teachers and a few more students raced out of the building.

Miss Gold rushed over to me, Danny, and Tina. "Kids, are you all right?" she asked.

We nodded.

Miss Gold appeared very upset. Her face was pale, and her hands were shaking.

She really cares about us, I realized.

"Thank goodness," Miss Gold breathed. "When I heard that fire alarm go off, I really got scared. Luckily there weren't many students left in the building. Mrs. Cooke, the principal, is still inside, checking every room."

I saw Anthony hovering around the edge of the crowd. I hurried over to him.

"Anthony, it's so weird," I said. "You always seem to be around when something bad happens."

His jaw dropped. "What? You think I had something to do with this?"

"I saw you outside the kitchen. What were you doing there?" I demanded.

"Nothing!" he insisted. "My locker happens to be outside the kitchen. I saw you guys baking cookies, and I was thinking maybe I'd help."

I narrowed my eyes at him. Anthony Gonzales, offer to help? Yeah, right.

It was just too weird. Someone scrawls THE CARNIVAL IS DOOMED all over the chalkboard — and Anthony walks by with chalk dust on his hands.

Someone smashes up the art projects — except for Anthony's painting.

36

A fire breaks out while we're baking — and Anthony just happens to be hanging around nearby.

Whenever something bad happens, Anthony is there.

Mrs. Cooke came out of the building. "The fire is out," she announced. "There wasn't too much damage, and no one was hurt. Everything is all right now."

"Thank goodness." Miss Gold sighed.

I felt nervous as I walked home. Did someone start that fire on purpose? I wondered.

It's strange, I thought. The only people in the kitchen were me, Tina, and Danny — the heads of the carnival.

What if someone isn't just trying to stop the carnival? I thought. What if someone is trying to hurt us?

When I got home, Mom and Amanda were watching the news. Mom stood in front of the TV, her purse slung over her arm. A reporter was interviewing Mrs. Cooke about the fire.

"Beth!" Mom hugged me. "I was just about to go to school and get you! I'm so glad you're all right!"

"I'm okay, Mom," I told her. "No one got hurt."

Mom sank onto the couch. "Thank goodness."

I wandered out to the back porch to check on Chirpy.

Chirpy fluttered his one good wing when he saw me.

"How are you feeling today?" I reached into the cage and gently rubbed his back. He fluttered again, weakly.

I gave him some birdseed. He ate a few seeds from my hand, then settled down to rest.

He doesn't look much better, I thought sadly. "Come on, Chirpy," I said. "Cheer up. Try to get strong again."

He pecked at another seed. "That's good," I said. "Keep eating."

I headed to my room. I felt totally wrecked. What a crazy week!

I sat down on my bed and took off my shoes. Suddenly I heard a noise.

THUMP.

I froze. What was that?

CLUNK.

It came from inside my closet!

I stared at the closet door. My heart pounded.

Calm down, I told myself. There's no one there.

No one is in my closet, I thought.

I sat frozen on my bed, listening.

THUD.

I gasped.

The carnival is doomed.

The words flashed into my mind.

Someone's after me! I thought. Someone has come to get me!

I heard breathing behind the closet door.

"Who's that?" I cried. "Who's in there?"

10

The closet door cracked open.

My heart raced. "Wh-who is it?" I asked again.

I waited, frozen in place.

The door creaked.

It swung open.

Amanda leaped out. She tackled me on the bed.

"Get off me!" I cried.

She tumbled to the floor.

"You scared me to death!" I shrieked.

"I know!" she replied gleefully. "I *wanted* to scare you!"

"Why?" I demanded.

"Because you never pay any attention to me," she sniffed.

"I've been busy!" I shouted, furious. "I can't help it! I can't spend every second playing with you!"

Amanda's upper lip trembled. "You used to *like* playing with me," she whined. "Now you're hardly ever home!"

I sighed. She's right, I realized. I've been so busy with the carnival I haven't spent any time with her. But still — she can't expect me to drop everything for her all the time.

"I'm sorry, Amanda," I said. "It's just that . . . things have been so crazy the last few days."

"I know." She nodded sadly. "But I miss you."

"Amanda, I promise to spend more time with you as soon as the carnival is over. That's tomorrow. You can wait one day, can't you?"

"You'll help me with my Barbies?" she asked.

"Yes. And anything else you want to do. I'll even take you to the petting zoo."

She brightened up. "Okay."

"And tomorrow night I'll take you to the carnival. That will be fun, won't it?"

"Uh-huh."

"Do you feel better now?"

She nodded. "Yeah."

"And you won't play any more mean tricks on me?"

"No. I promise." Did she have her fingers crossed? I couldn't see.

She waved good-bye and shut the door behind her.

I pulled off my socks. She's really not so bad, I thought. For an obnoxious little sister, I mean.

I decided to read for a while. I pulled down the covers and slid into bed.

I felt a little uncomfortable. I shifted.

Something strange touched my leg.

What *is* that? I wondered.

I moved my leg. Something touched it again.

Something cold.

"Yuck!" I groaned. I leaped out of bed and pulled down the covers.

The cow eyeball!

"Ohhh!"

Amanda's cow eyeball rolled along my sheets, leaving a slimy trail.

My stomach clenched. Then I heard peals of high-pitched giggling from my sister's room.

"Amanda, you're going to get it!" I shouted.

She's so horrible! I thought angrily. Why do I bother trying to be nice to her?

"I don't believe it!" Danny said. It was the next day. Tina, Danny, and I were on our way to the gym after school. "Tonight is the carnival. And nothing has gone wrong today."

"So far," I reminded him.

We were carrying projects from the art room to the gym. It was time to finish setting up the carnival.

The carnival is doomed, I thought. I couldn't get those words out of my head.

Would they come true? Was something terrible about to happen?

"Everybody heard about the oven fire," Tina said. "Lots of people baked cookies and stuff at home and brought them in. We might even have more food than last year!"

"That's great," I said. "The food tables make the most money."

I put down the paintings I was carrying and opened the door to the gym.

I thought I saw someone. Just a flash of blond hair. The figure darted out the back exit.

"Who was that?" I asked.

"Who?" Danny said. "I didn't see anyone."

"Neither did I," Tina said.

I shrugged and picked up the paintings. "Maybe I'm imagining things," I said.

"I'm going to run back to the art room to get some more stuff," Danny told us.

"Don't forget the masking tape," Tina reminded him.

Danny nodded and hurried out of the gym.

Tina led the way to the food tables. "Look at all the stuff people brought," she said happily.

The tables were loaded with dishes covered in tinfoil.

I'm hungry, I thought. I think I'll sneak a brownie while Tina's not looking.

I drifted over to the end of the table. I lifted the tinfoil off a plate and snatched a brownie.

I stuffed the brownie into my mouth.

I chewed. Something crunched.

What was that? A walnut?

I made a face. It didn't taste like a nut. It tasted sour.

I crunched again. And felt something crawl across my tongue.

Something was *alive* in my mouth!

I spit out the brownie.

"Ohh . . ." I moaned. "I'm going to be sick."

I dropped to my knees as my stomach heaved, and I vomited all over the floor.

11

"What? What is it?" Tina raced over to see what was wrong.

I finally stopped heaving and backed away. I covered my mouth with one hand.

We both stared down at the brownie. Tiny white wriggling maggots.

Tina squealed with terror. My stomach lurched again. I could still feel the maggots crawling over my tongue. Gagging, I hurried to the water fountain and frantically rinsed out my mouth.

Tina was checking every plate of food. "Who did this?" she demanded. "Who?"

I tried to reply but gagged again.

Maggots. I had maggots in my mouth! I'll never be normal again, I decided.

"What should we do?" Tina asked.

"We'd better tell Miss Gold," I suggested. "Maybe she'll know what to do."

Miss Gold bit her lip when we told her what had happened.

"Maggots," she murmured. "Maggots . . ."

She began to shake. Lines seemed to grow on her face right before my eyes. She sank into a chair and dropped her head into her hands.

"I think we should call off the carnival," she said quietly.

I gasped. "But-but —" Tina sputtered. "We worked so hard on it!"

"I know, girls." Miss Gold looked so frightened. "But I have a very bad feeling."

Tina and I glanced at each other. "Maybe she's right," I said. "A lot of bad things have happened. And they keep getting worse!"

"I don't know," Tina protested. "We've worked so hard. What else could go wrong?"

"A lot," Miss Gold said grimly.

She's really scared, I thought. "What do you mean?" I asked her.

Before she could reply, Anthony rushed in to the classroom.

"Hey — the dunking tank is all set up," he announced. "Want to see it? Danny is going to try it out."

Miss Gold frowned. I glanced at the black ring

on her finger. It glowed in the light from the window.

She saw me staring at it and covered it with her hand.

"Let's go see the dunking tank," she said, standing up.

We all trooped back to the gym.

"Hey!" Danny called. He sat on a bench at the top of the dunking machine, hovering over a tankful of water. Beside him stood a red-and-white target.

"I always wanted to try one of these," Danny said. "But Anthony will never dunk me."

"Oh, yeah?" Anthony grabbed three softballs and prepared to throw. If one of the balls hit the target, Danny would fall into the water.

"Anthony, be careful," Miss Gold warned.

"Don't worry, Miss Gold," Anthony assured her. "I won't clonk him in the head.

"Ready?" he called to Danny.

Danny yawned. "No way I'm getting wet."

Anthony gripped a ball. He wound up like a pitcher and hurled the ball at the target.

It bounced off the wall behind the dunking tank.

Danny laughed. "Missed me!"

"Anthony, that's enough," Miss Gold ordered. She was trying to sound tough, but her voice quavered. "We've seen how it works. Danny — climb out of there!" she called.

"No way, Miss Gold," Anthony said. "I've got

two more chances. And this time I'm not going to miss!"

He wound up again and threw. The ball just nipped the edge of the target.

"You throw like a girl!" Danny taunted.

"What's that supposed to mean?" I cried.

"Watch this!" Anthony picked up the third ball.

"Anthony — don't," Miss Gold warned. "Don't dunk him. He — he'll get his clothes all wet."

"Tough," Anthony muttered. "He asked for it." He wound up and pitched the ball.

BANG! It hit the target square in the middle.

SPLASH! Danny dropped into the tank of water.

"Aaaauuuggghh!" Danny let out a cry and began to thrash wildly in the water.

"Let me out!" he shrieked. "Help me! Help!"

At first I thought he was clowning around. But then I saw that his face was bright red.

"Help — somebody!"

It took us all so long to realize that he was in pain. But then I saw the steam rising up from the water.

And Danny moaned, "Boiling. It's boiling me!"

His eyes shut. His body went limp. And he sank under the water.

12

We raced to the tank. Climbed over the side.

Steam rose up around us. Boiling hot.

"Give us your hand!" Miss Gold screamed.

But Danny had passed out. He couldn't hear us.

We grabbed him by the shoulders and hoisted him up.

"Is he drowned?" Anthony cried. "Is he breathing?"

The custodian, Mr. Greaves, rushed into the gym, followed by his assistant, Jerry. They helped us pull Danny out.

We set him down on the floor. His skin was an angry red. He was breathing.

"The water —" he gasped. "It was so hot!"

I touched Danny's arm. It was boiling hot and red as a lobster.

"That's impossible!" Mr. Greaves insisted. "I just filled that tank with *cold* water. I swear!"

"Take him to the nurse's office — quick!" Miss Gold ordered.

Mr. Greaves helped Danny up and half-walked, half-carried him out of the gym.

"Man, I'm so sorry," Anthony said. "I didn't know that water was hot — I really didn't!"

Miss Gold's lip trembled. "Something dreadful is going to happen tonight — I just know it!"

"Miss Gold —" I asked. "How do you know?"

She rubbed her temples as if they ached. "I just know."

I hugged my knees to my chest. "What can we do?"

Miss Gold stood up. "Come with me, Beth. We're going to the principal's office to ask her to call off the carnival."

"That was the nurse," Mrs. Cooke announced, hanging up the phone. Miss Gold and I had been sitting in her office when the phone rang. "She said Danny will be fine."

Mrs. Cooke folded her hands on her desk and frowned at us. "I understand your concerns, Miss Gold. I wish I could call off the carnival. But it's too late."

Miss Gold stared down at the black ring on her hand. She looked very upset.

"We'll just have to take extra care," Mrs. Cooke

continued. "I'll call the police and ask them to send someone to keep an eye on things. That should help."

"Thank you, Mrs. Cooke." Miss Gold and I left the office.

"Are you all right, Miss Gold?" I asked.

She clasped her hand over the ring.

She didn't answer my question. Instead, she took off, running down the hall, vanishing around the corner.

"I don't want any dinner, Mom," Amanda declared. "I'm going to eat at the carnival tonight — right, Beth?"

I swallowed, thinking of the maggot-covered brownies. "Um — I don't know, Amanda," I began. "I'm not sure they'll have anything good there."

"Sure they will!" Amanda cried. "They always do!"

"I guess you can have hot dogs for dinner once in a while," Mom agreed. "Or whatever they're serving this year."

My stomach turned over again. Chocolate-covered maggots, anyone?

"I guess they have hot dogs," I replied. "And other stuff."

"I can't wait to go," Amanda said. "And you'd better not try to back out of taking me, Beth. Remember — you promised."

"I know." I felt miserable. Amanda would kill me if I refused to take her to the carnival. But something inside told me she shouldn't go.

"Come on," I said, tugging Amanda's hand. "Let's get this over with."

13

"I guess Miss Gold was wrong," Tina said. "So far, the carnival is going great!"

Amanda and I stood in front of Tina's food table. We watched crowds of people streaming into the carnival, laughing and spending lots of money on food and games and other activities.

"I threw out all the maggoty food," Tina told us. "My dad and I had an emergency bake session this afternoon. We don't have as much stuff to sell as before — but at least it doesn't have bugs in it! Yuck!"

I peered closely at a chocolate chip cookie. No sign of bugs — but I decided not to take any chances.

"I'll have two sugar cookies," Amanda ordered.

"One dollar," Tina said.

I paid Tina and Amanda took the cookies. "Mmm!" she cried, biting into one. "Yummy."

Amanda and I strolled past the art sale. Parents crowded the booth, buying their kids' stuff.

I waved at Elizabeth Gordon, who was working at the booth. "Everything going okay?" I asked her.

"Yes. Awesome." She smiled. "Oliver wanted me to tell you it's your turn to do ticket-taking," she added. "His shift is over."

"Okay." I turned to Amanda. "Will you be all right on your own for a little while? I've got to take tickets at the door."

"I'll keep an eye on her." Anthony suddenly appeared behind us.

I hesitated. I wasn't sure I wanted to leave Amanda with Anthony. But I figured it was better than leaving her alone.

"Don't worry, I won't toss her in the dunking tank," he promised.

"Ha ha. I'll be okay, Beth," Amanda assured me.

"Well . . . all right. But if you need me, Amanda, I'll be at the front entrance. Okay?"

"Whatever," she said impatiently.

I sighed and walked to the gym entrance. Oliver Slivka stood up at the ticket table.

"Finally," he groaned. "You were supposed to take over half an hour ago."

"Sorry, Oliver." I sat down behind the cash box. "Thanks for helping."

I nodded to the policeman standing just outside the gym doors. Mrs. Cooke had hired extra security for the carnival, just in case.

As people arrived, I sold them tickets. All the while I tried to keep an eye out for Amanda and Anthony.

I saw Amanda at the basketball toss game.

Where's Anthony? I wondered. I didn't see him.

It's just like him to offer to watch Amanda and then disappear.

The next time I checked, Amanda had won a huge stuffed bear at the ring toss booth. She headed toward the face-painting tables.

I guess she's okay, I decided.

Kids in the school band climbed onto the stage to give a concert. I searched for Amanda. She was busy having her face painted.

Still no sign of Anthony, I thought, annoyed. Where did he go?

Suddenly, the gym lights dimmed. I gasped. What's happening? I wondered.

I glanced up as a tall figure stepped into the gym.

He wore a long gray robe. His face was hidden by a large hood.

I strained to see the face behind the hood. "Um — admission is one dollar," I said.

The mysterious figure didn't seem to hear me.

I held out a ticket. "One dollar, please."

He raised both arms. I gasped again as the lights in the gym flashed on and off.

People cried out in surprise. The band stopped playing.

The air suddenly grew cold. I shivered.

The robed figure pushed past me, walking stiffly. "Hey!" I cried. "Stop!"

He ignored me. People turned to stare at him, terrified.

"Stop!" I yelled again.

The stranger began to twirl. Round and round, faster and faster. The gym lights flashed off and on, off and on.

What's happening? I thought. Who *is* that?

I felt as if I were spinning too. Faster and faster, round and round.

Whoa. I clutched my head, feeling dizzy.

The whole gym is spinning! I realized. Just like the stranger, faster and faster.

What's he doing? I thought, terrified. "Stop him!" I shrieked. *"Stop him!"*

14

I stared dizzily through the haze of blinking lights. Everyone in the gym seemed stunned, unable to move.

"Get him!" I repeated weakly.

The stranger stopped spinning and stabbed the air with both hands.

The lights blinked faster. The gym doors slammed shut with a loud *BOOM*.

A low hum buzzed through the air. It grew louder and louder, until finally the hum became a roar. The roar of a speeding plane about to crash.

What's that sound? I thought, staring around the room.

The floor of the gym shook. People tumbled to the ground. I struggled to keep my balance.

"No!" I cried. "Please! Please!"

The water splashed up from the dunking tank and swept over the gym like a tidal wave. People were screaming now — screaming and running for cover. I dove across the gym as the water washed over my feet.

I saw the food table ahead of me. Tina cowered behind it.

I'll jump on top of it, I decided.

I splashed across the gym floor. Just as I was about to leap, the food table suddenly burst into flames.

"Help!" Tina screamed, stumbling away. People were scurrying in all directions, screaming and crying in panic.

I headed toward the basketball booth. Right before I reached it, it exploded!

Screams echoed through the gym. The air filled with smoke. I've got to find Amanda, I realized

"Amanda!" I shouted. "Amanda! Where are you?"

The gym rocked and tossed like a boat on the ocean.

I stumbled across the floor, trying to keep my balance.

"Amanda!" I screamed again.

Another buzz. Something dove toward my head. I ducked.

Wasps! The gym was swarming with wasps. They buzzed through the air, darting and diving.

People shrieked as the wasps attacked.

An angry swarm of wasps surrounded me like a dark cloud.

"Noooo!" A scream escaped my throat. I covered my head and tried to run away from them.

The swarm stuck with me. I scooped a handful of water off the wet floor and tried to splash them away.

The wasps buzzed off to attack someone else.

"Get me out of here!" a man pleaded. He threw himself against the door and banged on it furiously.

It wouldn't open. It was locked!

People piled up against the door, pushing and shoving.

"Let us out!" they shouted.

Another game booth exploded into flames.

I scanned the gym for my little sister. And spotted her cowering against the back wall, surrounded by wasps. She was screaming and covering her head.

"Amanda!" I called over the deafening noise. "I'm coming!"

I dove across the gym floor. Panicking people blocked my way. I shoved them aside. I had to reach Amanda.

I saw the hooded stranger ahead of me. He glided across the floor. Nothing bothered him — not the wasps, or the rocking, spinning gym, or the flames dancing over the room.

He just kept moving — heading straight for Amanda!

I had to get to her first. My way was blocked by the face-painting table.

I crawled over the table. I jumped off.
The table burst into flames.

I dodged the fire.

Too late.

The hooded figure grabbed Amanda — and lifted her off the floor.

"No!" I shrieked. "Let her go!"

Amanda screamed in terror.

The stranger swung her high — and carried her away.

15

Amanda's voice sounded so tiny over the cries of the crowd. "Beth — help! Help me!"

I've got to save her! I thought. I raced to the back of the gym and threw myself at the stranger, trying to tackle him.

Missed!

I belly-flopped to the floor. The stranger stood a few feet behind me, Amanda over his shoulder.

How did he dodge me so quickly? I wondered, jumping to my feet.

People were shouting and crying, running in all directions. The stranger pressed through the crowd, carrying Amanda halfway across the gym.

"Beth!" Amanda screamed. "Stop him!" She pounded on the stranger's back. It had no effect on him.

I chased them again. As I ran, the policeman burst through the front doors. People flooded outside.

"Help!" I shouted to the policeman. I waved to him from the back of the gym. The stranger stood between me and the policeman, heading for the doors.

"Stop him!" I called to the policeman. "He's got my sister!"

The policeman sped toward the stranger and tackled him.

But the stranger slipped out of his grasp — like air.

Then the stranger appeared behind the policeman, Amanda over his shoulder.

He's heading for the doors! I thought, panicking. I raced toward them. But so many people blocked my way!

"Stop him!" I screamed. "He's taking my sister!"

The policeman jumped to his feet and whirled around. He dove at the stranger again — and knocked him down. Amanda tumbled to the floor.

The policeman pinned down the stranger. Amanda rushed into my arms.

"Beth!" she sobbed. "I-I'm so scared!"

I held her. The policeman handcuffed the stranger.

Then he pulled off the stranger's hood.

"No!" I gasped. "Not *you*!"

16

I stared in shock as the hood slid back —
revealing Miss Gold.

Her blonde hair shone in the light. The black
ring flashed on her finger.

Her eyes rolled around in their sockets.

"It wasn't me!" she shrieked. "I swear it wasn't
me!"

Huh? What is she saying? I wondered.

The ring flashed again.

The police began to lead Miss Gold away. She
screamed and thrashed, trying to pull free.

Stunned, I hugged Amanda tighter.

It must have been Miss Gold all along, I realized. All the terrible things that happened — *she*
did them!

But why? And how? How did she do all those frightening things?

It was almost ... not human, I realized. The ground shaking, the lights flashing, the wasps attacking ...

What happened to her? I wondered. She always seemed so nice. How could she be so evil?

I had to find some answers. I knew if I didn't, it would bother me for the rest of my life.

I let go of Amanda and raced out of the gym. The police had just locked Miss Gold in the backseat of their car.

"Wait!" I shouted.

Too late.

They didn't hear me. They sped away.

Something flashed on the sidewalk in front of me. I bent down to pick it up.

The black ring!

Did she drop it? Did she throw it away?

I stared into the black jewel. The evil face glared out at me.

I couldn't stop staring at it. Staring ... staring. And then something made me slip the ring on my finger.

I shook my head, trying to clear my mind. What am I doing? I asked myself.

I tried to pull off the ring.

But I felt it tighten around my finger.

No! I yanked on it again.

No! I thought. It's stuck! So tight now ... so tight.

I raised the shiny jewel and stared at the smoky face inside.

My heart froze.

The face appeared to be laughing.

Why?

17

"This always works." Mom was greasing my ring finger with butter.

"I hope so," I muttered. I'd already tried soaking my finger in cold water and tugging until my finger was red and sore.

Mom tried to slide the ring off. It stuck at the knuckle.

"Beth, how did you get this thing on?" Mom demanded. "It's too small to fit over your knuckle!"

"I know," I sighed.

Mom yanked on the ring. No use.

"Isn't there anything else we can try?" I pleaded. "Axle grease? Olive oil? Anything?"

"I'll try to think of something." Mom stared at my finger, puzzled. "Maybe your finger is swollen from all the tugging we've done. Let it sit for a while."

I don't want to let it sit, I thought, twisting the ring.

The face in the jewel stared out at me.

I want to get this ring off — *now*!

Miss Gold got it off somehow, I thought, rubbing the black band.

Maybe she can tell me how she did it.

"Beth! Mom!" Amanda called from the living room. "The school carnival is on the news!"

Mom and I rushed into the living room to watch. A reporter stood in the wreckage of the gym, interviewing parents and teachers.

They all seemed frightened and baffled. Mrs. Cooke, the principal, said, "I apologize to everyone. But I can't explain it. It seems one of our sixth-grade teachers was having emotional problems. But she showed no sign of it . . ."

"Because of the incident, Marchfield Middle School will be closed for the rest of the week," the reporter announced. "The teacher, Miss Melanie Gold, was taken to Marchfield Hospital for testing."

I glanced at Mom. I knew she would never want me to see Miss Gold. Not after what happened at the carnival.

Mom would say it was too dangerous. After all, Miss Gold had gone crazy.

But I had to see her. I had to find out what had

happened to her. Why she had done so many terrible things.

"It's very late, girls," Mom said, switching off the TV. "And you've had an upsetting evening. I think we should all go to bed."

She dragged herself off the couch. She kissed Amanda good night, then me. I watched her go into the kitchen to turn on the dishwasher.

I went out to the back porch to say good night to Chirpy. I tried to feed him some seeds, but he wouldn't eat. He doesn't seem to be getting better, I thought sadly.

Tomorrow, I vowed. Tomorrow I'll sneak down to the hospital and see Miss Gold.

Maybe she can help me get the ring off. And maybe she can explain what happened today.

I went to bed late that night. I fell into a strange, restless sleep, haunted by dreams.

"It's dark," I murmured to myself. "It's so dark. . . ."

I stepped forward — and crashed into a wall. Everything was pitch-black. I couldn't see at all.

I slid my hands along the wall. It felt slippery, like butter.

I'm in a maze, I realized. I have to feel my way through.

But where am I going? I wondered. What's at the end of the maze?

I stumbled through blindly. My hands were coated with grease.

At last I could see. I stood in the gym, surrounded by ducks. Only, instead of duck heads, they all had human heads.

One duck head looked exactly like Danny Jacobs. The next one looked like Tina Crowley. Another duck was Anthony Gonzales.

"This isn't right!" I screamed. "Your heads don't belong on duck bodies!"

I grabbed the Anthony duck and tore its head off. Blood gushed from its neck. Feathers flew into the air.

"Ha ha ha ha!" I laughed. I splashed my hand in the blood and rubbed it on the black ring.

"This will get the ring off!" I cackled. "Blood will take it off!

"No!" I sat up. I blinked.

My room was just beginning to get light. Dawn.

What a weird dream, I thought. I touched my face. It was burning hot. My nightshirt clung wetly to my back.

Why am I sweating? I wondered. Why did I have so many weird dreams last night?

I squinted at the black ring. The smoky face inside seemed to gaze out at me.

I shuddered.

It seemed to stare into my eyes. As if it were trying to read something there.

"Beth?"

I gasped, startled. Amanda stood in the doorway.

"What?" I cried. "What are you doing up?"

"Beth — why did you do that?" Amanda asked.

"Huh? Do what?"

The room slowly grew lighter. I gazed around.

Oh, no, I thought.

Did I do that?

Feathers floated in the air. Feathers covered the floor, my desk, my chair, my bed.

My pillows had been ripped apart — as if a wild animal had torn them to shreds.

18

"**B**eth, what is your problem?" Mom scolded. "It looks like a monster tore through here!"

I was beginning to clean my room when Mom got up.

"It's just feathers." I tried to make it sound like nothing weird had happened. "It's no big deal."

Mom studied a shredded piece of pillowcase. "It's not like you, Beth. You've never done anything like this before."

I know, I thought. Tell me about it.

"I did it in my sleep." I tried to keep my voice steady. "I was having a nightmare."

She gazed at me with that worried look she gets. I plugged in the vacuum cleaner.

"Beth — the carnival last night. Is there anything you want to talk —"

I didn't hear the rest of what she said. I drowned her out with the vacuum cleaner.

That afternoon I rode my bike downtown to Marchfield Hospital.

I slipped upstairs and asked a nurse where Miss Gold was staying.

"She's in this ward," the nurse told me. "Do you have flowers or a card for her?"

"No," I replied. "I need to see her."

"I'm sorry," the nurse said. "No one is allowed to see her. Doctor's orders."

"I'm one of her students," I protested. "I've got to see her. Just for a minute."

"Absolutely not." The nurse frowned. "If you want to leave her a card or something, I'll see that she gets it." She turned away to answer the phone.

I stared down the long hallway. Door after door after door, and they all looked alike.

I wish I knew her room number, I thought. Then maybe I could sneak in and see her.

I tried to peek at the charts on the nurse's desk. Maybe I could glimpse Miss Gold's room number there.

I stood on tiptoe, reading upside down. I didn't see any room numbers.

The nurse hung up the phone. "Please don't hang around here, miss."

"I want to give Miss Gold a card," I told her. "I'll be back in a minute."

I raced downstairs to the gift shop and bought a get-well card. I signed my name and took it back up to Miss Gold's ward. I held it up to the nurse.

"Fine. I'll see she gets it." The nurse didn't even look up. She was busy filling out a form.

"Please give it to her *now*," I insisted. "It's important."

The nurse lifted her head and glared at me. She snatched up the card and stormed down the hallway. I watched carefully to see which room she went into.

It was the last room on the left. I noticed an exit door at the end of the hall.

I'll bet there's a stairwell behind that door, I thought.

I hurried back downstairs. I strode down the hall as if I knew where I was going. As if I belonged there.

Nobody stopped me.

At the end of the hall stood an exit door. Just like the one outside Miss Gold's room. I opened it and sneaked up the stairs.

On the next floor I carefully cracked open the door. The nurse was marching back to her station.

The coast was clear.

I slipped out of the stairwell. I darted across the hall and through the last door on the left.

Miss Gold lay quietly on the bed. The room was dimly lit — the curtains were closed.

I shut the door behind me. Miss Gold turned her head.

"Beth," she said weakly. She waved the card I'd just bought and added, "Thank you."

I slowly approached the bed. Miss Gold looked terrible. I remembered how her eyes used to be so sparkly and blue. But now they looked gray and dead.

"Miss Gold," I began. "What happened to you?"

She stared up at me. Now her eyes were blank.

"Last night — at the gym —" I prompted her. "Why did you do it?"

She closed her eyes. "I don't know, Beth. I can't explain it."

"But — did you do everything?" I asked. "The writing on the chalkboard? Smashing up the art room? Everything?"

She blinked her eyes open. "I — I suppose I did." She didn't seem too sure. "I can hardly believe it myself."

I twisted the black ring on my finger. "I found something of yours outside the gym. I brought it for you."

I held up my left hand. The black ring sparkled.

Miss Gold's face twisted in shock. "Beth — no! What are you doing with that?"

"I told you — I found it . . ."

She grabbed my hand and desperately tugged at the ring. "Take it off! Take it off right now!" she ordered. She pulled so hard, my finger throbbed with pain.

"I can't!" I cried. "I was hoping you could help me!"

She yanked on the ring as hard as she could. At last she let her hands drop helplessly into her lap.

"Get that thing away from me!" she rasped. "Get it away! And get it off your finger as soon as you can! I'm warning you!"

I began to shake. "Miss Gold, please —"

"Get out now!" she demanded. "I can't help you. Just get rid of that ring!"

Trembling, I staggered out of the room. I slipped down the staircase and ran outside into the bright spring sunshine.

I jumped on my bike and pedaled home as fast as I could. *"Get rid of the ring! Get rid of the ring!"* I chanted to myself as I rode.

I dumped my bike in the garage and flew into the house. *"Get rid of the ring,"* I told myself. *"Get rid of the ring."*

I stopped in the kitchen, panting. The ring caught the light and flashed.

I gazed at the black jewel.

The face stared out at me. Its eyes seemed to drill into mine.

I couldn't take my eyes off that face. I couldn't tear myself away from that deep stare.

A calm feeling began to sweep over me. It's

okay, I thought. Everything is okay. There's nothing to worry about.

I relaxed as the calmness washed over me.

I feel so much better now, I realized. So much happier and calmer.

What a beautiful ring.

19

"**R**emember, Beth — you promised."

Amanda and I were walking to school. It was Monday morning, a few days after the carnival. Amanda was back to her usual pesty self.

"Yes, I remember," I said. "I promise I'll help you arrange your stupid Barbies tonight."

Amanda scowled. "Don't call them stupid! I won't let you help if you call them that."

"I don't *want* to help you, stupid," I snapped.

I paused. The words sounded funny to me.

I'd never called Amanda stupid before. Strange.

"I'll only play with you if you let me name them," I went on. "I'll call them Dopey, Airhead, Space Case, Brainless . . ."

"But one of my Barbies is a doctor!" Amanda protested. "You can't call her Brainless!"

"Okay, I won't. I'll call her Doctor Dumb-Dumb."

Amanda fumed as we plodded down the street.

We were just passing Danny's house when he appeared. "Hey, Beth — wait up!" he called.

"Hi, *Danny*," Amanda cooed, making goo-goo eyes at him. I kicked her in the shin.

"Ow!" she protested. But it worked. It shut her up.

"I wonder what school will be like today," Danny said to me. "I mean, after what happened at the carnival." He paused.

"I guess we'll have a substitute teacher for a while," I said.

"Did you hear about the bike-a-thon?" he asked.

I shook my head.

"It's for charity," he explained. "You get sponsors, and you have to ride ten miles. It's this Saturday. Want to do it with me?"

"Definitely!" I exclaimed.

He finally asked me to do something outside of school!

"Great!" Danny said. "I've got an extra entry form in my backpack. I'll give it to you when we get to school."

Suddenly I heard the squeal of bike brakes behind me. Before I could turn around, something bumped me hard.

"Ow!" I cried. I spun around. "Anthony!"

"Whoops. Sorry." Anthony didn't look sorry at

all. He was grinning behind his dark, expensive sunglasses.

He bumped into me on purpose! I realized. "Grow up, Anthony!" I cried angrily. "You're not funny."

"Who says?" Anthony replied. "I think I'm hilarious."

I rolled my eyes.

"Hey, Anthony — are you doing the bike-a-thon this Saturday?" Danny asked.

"No way," Anthony replied. "Why would I want to bike ten miles?"

"*I'm* biking in it," I told him.

"You *would*," he snapped. "You're such a goody-goody."

Amanda snickered. I kicked her in the shin again.

She shut up. I ought to do that more often, I thought.

"Here's your school, Amanda." We stopped at the elementary school. "I'll see you this afternoon."

"Remember — the Barbies!" she called as she ran into the building.

"You still play with Barbies?" Anthony teased. "I knew you were babyish, but —"

I felt my face get hot. Why did Anthony have to be so mean to me? Especially in front of Danny?

"Baby Bethy, the goody-goody," Anthony taunted.

I stole a glance at Danny. He ran a few steps ahead and kicked a rock into the street.

Two blocks later we arrived at school. Anthony rode around to the side of the building and parked his bike. He and Danny started inside.

"You guys go ahead," I told them. "I'm going to wait for Tina. I told her I'd meet her out front."

"Okay. See you."

The first bell rang. I hurried around to the side of the school building.

Anthony's bike, green and shiny, glistened in the sunlight.

He sure loves that bike, I thought.

Too bad.

I felt a surge of power shoot through my body.

I grabbed the chain that locked the bike and ripped it off. I tore it into pieces and tossed them to the ground.

I had no idea I was so strong! I thought. It's almost as if I have superpowers!

I yanked off the front wheel and bent it in half. Then I crushed the back wheel.

I left the mangled bike where I'd found it.

Wait until Anthony sees *that*, I thought gleefully.

And he thought I was a goody-goody.

I glanced back at the wrecked bike as I headed to the door.

I can't believe *I* did that, I thought.

I've never felt so strong. I actually bent the wheel of a bike!

How did I do it? I asked myself. How?

20

The second bell rang. I hurried into the school building.

Kids were just filing in when I reached the classroom. A short, bald man with glasses and a bow tie sat behind the desk. On the chalkboard behind him he'd written his name — MR. CHARLES.

He patted a strand of hair over his bald spot. Then he straightened his bow tie. Oh, great, I thought. He looks like loads of fun.

I dropped my books on my desk. I noticed Anthony's sunglasses lying on his desk across the room.

He must have gone to his locker, I realized.

I crossed the room and snatched up the sunglasses. I glanced around.

No one was watching.

I stashed the glasses in my pocket. Then I grabbed my history textbook. It was the heaviest book I had.

And I headed for the bathroom.

I checked under the stalls to see if anybody was in there. The bathroom was empty.

I placed the sunglasses on the windowsill. With one quick *BANG!* I smashed the book down on them.

And crushed them to bits. The cracking sound made me laugh.

I brushed the broken pieces into my hand and carried them back to the classroom. Anthony hadn't returned to his desk yet.

I took another look around. Nobody watching.

I sprinkled the tiny pieces of plastic and glass on top of Anthony's desk.

Maybe you won't feel so cool without your shades, huh, Anthony? I thought, snickering.

A few minutes later, Anthony returned to the classroom. He stared curiously at the strange pile on his desk.

He fingered a few of the pieces. Then his jaw dropped.

"Who did this?" he demanded. He threw accusing glances at the kids sitting around him. "Who broke my shades?"

The other kids shrugged. "Didn't you see anything?" he asked. "Didn't you see who did it?" He glared at David Kelly, who sat behind him.

"*I* didn't do it," David insisted.

"Young man, take your seat please." Mr. Charles stood at the front of the room with a roll book.

"Somebody smashed my sunglasses!" Anthony wailed. "I want to know who did it!"

"You can worry about that after class," Mr. Charles said. "Now, please sit down."

Anthony grumbled as he dropped into his seat. He scowled at everyone around him.

Everyone but me, of course. He never thought *I* was the one who broke his sunglasses. Not for a minute.

Not goody-goody Beth.

It felt good, being bad. I'd never done anything so bad before in my life.

And suddenly, I liked it.

At recess, I roamed the halls, looking for trouble. It was warm and sunny, and almost everybody was outside.

Then I saw him. A fifth grader I didn't even know.

He was a small kid with greasy dark hair. His locker was open, and he was putting away some books.

I didn't even think about what I was going to do. I just did it.

I rushed at the boy and shoved him into his locker.

"Hey!" he yelped. "Stop —"

I slammed the door shut. He banged on it, screaming, "Stop it! Let me out! Let me out of here!"

I smiled to myself. Then I locked him inside.

21

I walked away and left him there.

I could hear him pounding and screaming as I strolled down the hall. It gave me a little thrill.

That was fun, I thought. Now on to the lunchroom.

I stood in line, waiting to fill up a tray with the usual cafeteria food. Then I noticed something near the door of the kitchen.

A mouse?

Yes. A mouse.

The mouse squeezed under the door and scampered into the kitchen. I pushed open the door and followed it in.

The kitchen workers were all busy serving the kids. I sneaked past them and into the huge pantry in back.

Aha. I spotted the mouse hiding behind a sack of rice in the corner. Quick as a cat, I scooped up the mouse before it even had a chance to squeak!

This is amazing, I thought. I've never been so quick before.

I sneaked back out to the cafeteria.

I'll bet this mouse is hungry, I thought. Maybe it would like a little soup.

When no one was looking, I dropped the mouse into a vat of vegetable soup.

"Eat up, kids!" I whispered.

I grabbed a tray and slowly moved through the line, waiting to see what would happen.

Tina Crowley and two of her friends entered the line.

First victims, I thought happily.

The lunch lady dipped her ladle into the vat of soup. She spooned it into a bowl and handed it to Tina.

Tina zipped through the line and sat down with her friends. I followed and perched nearby.

I watched Tina dip her spoon in the soup and bring it to her lips.

The mouse popped his head up and squeaked.

Tina's scream shook the walls.

I laughed.

The mouse squeaked again and did a breast-stroke across the soup bowl.

Tina screamed again. Her friends dropped their

trays and ran from the lunchroom, shrieking their heads off.

The whole room was in a panic. Dripping with soup, the mouse leaped off the table and scampered across the floor. Everybody looked so funny. The ladies who served the food were shrieking and swatting at the mouse.

Kids dropped their lunches and ran screaming out of the lunchroom.

Now I understand, I thought, as I watched the whole school turn upside down.

Now I know why Anthony is always doing mean things to people.

Because it's so much fun!

The house was empty when I got home that afternoon. Mom was at work.

Where's Amanda? I wondered. Then I remembered. She had a soccer game that afternoon.

So nobody's home, I thought, glancing around for something to do. Hmmm . . .

I think I'll go up to Amanda's room, I decided. I promised to help her arrange her Barbies, didn't I?

The Barbies lay in a tangled heap on Amanda's bed. These dolls really do need arranging, I thought. Maybe I should get started now.

Amanda will be so surprised when she gets home.

I picked up the first Barbie and examined it. This must be the Surfer Barbie, I realized.

"You won't be doing much surfing from now on, Surfer Barbie," I said.

I snapped one of her legs off. Then the other.

CRACK, CRACK. They made such a cool sound as I broke them off.

Then I tore off her arms. *CRACK, CRACK.*

I tossed the doll on the floor and picked up the next one. "You must be the Doctor Barbie," I said. "Okay, Doctor Barbie — see if you can heal this!"

CRACK, CRACK.

I love that sound, I thought.

I ripped the arms and legs off every single doll.

CRACK, CRACK.

And I laughed the whole time.

22

"**M**om!" Amanda's screams rang through the house. "Mom! Look what happened!"

I lay on my bed in my room, listening. Mom raced into Amanda's room. "What's wrong, honey?"

"Look!" Amanda shouted. "Somebody —" She started to sob. "S-somebody broke all my Barbies!"

I heard Mom gasp. "I — I don't know how . . ."

Amanda barged into my room. "Beth!" she demanded. "You did it! Why? Why did you do this to me?"

I sat up. "Me? I didn't do it!" I lied. "I never touched your Barbies!"

Mom appeared behind her. "Beth — that's not like you! Why would you do such a thing?"

"I told you!" I insisted. "I didn't do it! Really!"

Mom frowned.

"Then who did?" Amanda shrieked. "You were the only one here!" She sobbed, tears rolling down her cheeks.

Mom's eyes locked on mine. I knew she thought I broke Amanda's dolls. But at the same time, Mom couldn't believe I would do something like that.

She led Amanda away. "Come on, honey," she soothed. "Let's see if we can put them back together."

They returned to Amanda's room. I lay back against my pillows.

Why did I do that? I wondered. Why did I break Amanda's dolls?

I remembered doing it. I remembered doing lots of bad things that day. But I didn't know why.

Amanda sobbed in the next room. I heard Mom trying to comfort her.

I suddenly felt terrible. My whole body began to tremble.

What's happening to me? I wondered. I broke Anthony's bike and sunglasses. I put a mouse in Tina's soup.

I even locked a little kid in his locker! For no reason! I didn't even know him.

And then I ruined my sister's Barbies. All in one day.

What happened to me? I used to be so nice.

The black ring flashed on my finger.

The ring, I thought, gazing at it. Of course. The ring.

The ghostly face inside smiled out at me. I thought I saw it wink.

Somehow it's making me do evil things! I thought. Just like Miss Gold.

I shuddered.

This is just the beginning, I realized.

I remembered how nice Miss Gold once was.

But by the night of the carnival, she had completely changed.

She had supernatural powers. She tried to kill people! She tried to kill everyone in that gym!

My stomach knotted up. I felt sick.

What am *I* going to do?

How can I stop it?

I gripped the ring and tried to rip it off my finger. "Off!" I cried. "I've got to get it off!"

The evil face glared out at me.

It was as if he could read my thoughts — and I could read his.

Stop! he commanded. *You cannot remove the ring.*

I stopped.

This is only the beginning, he said. *Kid stuff. The real evil is still to come.*

Don't try to get rid of me. You can't do it.

Soon you won't even want to do it.

The ring is controlling me! I thought.

I felt a chill — as if my heart were slowly being covered with ice.

But what's going to happen? I wondered.

What if I keep getting more and more evil?

What am I going to do next?

I was eating breakfast on Saturday morning. Amanda sat across the table from me, eyeing me warily.

Bad things had happened to her all week. Someone tore up her homework. Someone replaced her favorite shampoo with corn oil. Someone put a couple of slugs in her spaghetti sauce.

That someone was me, of course. But I never admitted to any of the terrible things I did. "I didn't do it!" I claimed, over and over.

Amanda watched me from over her cereal bowl. She didn't know what to think.

I didn't know what to think, either.

I didn't want to do any of those things. But I did them anyway.

Amanda was lucky. I was much meaner to the kids at school.

One girl brought in her expensive new laptop computer. I poured soda all over it. It doesn't work anymore.

I set the class hamster loose — and then locked a stray cat in the room with him.

Danny, who always fed the hamster, found the hamster's mangled little body under a desk.

I hated myself for doing those things. But I couldn't stop myself!

I had no control.

Every day the ring's power over me grew stronger. And every day, my evil grew.

I finished my cereal and went out to the porch to check on Chirpy.

Poor Chirpy, I thought. He lay on the floor of his cage, breathing weakly. His broken wing was still bandaged.

"Come on, Chirpy — eat," I urged. I tried to stuff a few seeds into his beak. He didn't swallow them.

Someone knocked on the porch door. "Beth! You ready to go?"

"Hi, Danny." I opened the door. He leaned his bike against the wall and came in.

"Come on!" he cried. "You're not wearing that to the bike-a-thon, are you?"

I glanced down and realized I was still in my pajamas!

The bike-a-thon. Oh, no.

I can't go to the bike-a-thon, I thought. What if I do something really bad there?

What if I hurt somebody?

"Danny, I can't go," I said. "I — I'm sick. See — I'm still in my pajamas!"

"You're not sick." Danny didn't believe me. "Come on — you have to go! It's for charity! You can't let everybody down!"

"No, Danny, really. I'm not feeling well."

I can't go, I thought desperately. I can't!

There will be so many kids there. So many people to hurt.

So many ways to be evil.

I glanced down at the ring. If only I could get it off!

Every night before I went to sleep I tried and tried to pull the ring off.

And every night that evil face stared me down. *You can't escape,* he said.

"Who *are* you?" I asked the face in the ring.

He never answered.

How did he get inside the ring? I wondered.

Why does he want to make me hurt people?

He never told me. But whenever I tried to take off the ring, his voice echoed inside my head.

You are in my power now, he said.

And I knew it was true. So I tried to stay as far away from people as I could.

"I won't let you miss it," Danny insisted. "It will be fun! And besides, everyone is waiting for you!"

"Danny, I can't," I insisted. "Really. They'll get along without me."

Danny gazed at me with his big brown eyes. "Beth," he said quietly. "I never knew you were so selfish."

I lowered my head. The black ring caught my eye. The smoky face seemed to grin at me.

That's right, Beth. I heard his voice inside my head. *Go. Go . . .*

Danny pushed me into the house. "Get in there and put on your bike shorts. I'll wait for you right here."

I went inside.

"And hurry up!" Danny called.

I went up to my room and got dressed. Maybe everything will be okay, I thought. I'll just ride my bike. I'll be helping charity.

I *should* go, I realized. I'll fight the evil. I'm strong. I can resist it.

A few minutes later I grabbed my bike from the garage and met Danny out front.

"I knew you'd do it." Danny grinned at me.

We rode to Marchfield High School, where the bike-a-thon began. The school sat perched on top of a steep hill. I stared down the twisting, winding hill.

The first leg of the bike-a-thon would be tricky, I realized. All downhill — but lots of steep curves. It would be easy to wipe out down there, I thought.

Dozens of kids had gathered for the race. I knew some of them — they were from my school.

And then a last biker sped into the parking lot. He braked suddenly, spraying gravel everywhere.

Anthony?

"Hey, geeks!" he cried. "Are you losers doing this too?"

"I thought bike-a-thons were for goody-goodies," I reminded him.

"They are — sort of," Anthony replied. "But I've got a new bike, and I want to show it off."

I stared at his shiny, fancy new bike. It was sleek and black, and looked much faster than any other bike there.

"Some jerk wrecked my bike last week," Anthony said.

"Oh, really?" I said, looking away. "That's terrible."

"I still haven't found out who did it," he went on. "But whoever it was — I'm going to show him. I'm going to show him I'm not scared. And my new bike is even better than my old one. I'm going to come in first today."

"Good for you," I snapped.

A tall woman blew a whistle. "Kids! Kids! Gather around for a minute. I want to explain the rules to you."

Everyone left their bikes in the parking lot and gathered around the front steps of the school.

I hung back.

Anthony will be leading the pack down that hill, I decided.

If he wipes out, *everyone* will crash.

My heart began to pound with excitement.

There will lots of injuries, I thought. Lots of wonderful crashes.

Lots of screams.

How easy would it be to take the brakes off Anthony's bike?

I held the black ring in the sunlight. The evil face smiled at me.

Yes, it commanded. *Yes! Do it!*

The tall woman was pointing out the bike route on a big map. The other kids all listened carefully.

I slipped away from the group. I sneaked over to Anthony's bike.

I studied the hand brakes. All I have to do is snap off the cord, I decided.

Once Anthony starts down the hill, he won't be able to stop. He won't be able to slow down.

He'll speed to the bottom.

Then he'll crash. And all the kids behind him will smash right into him.

They'll all crash too.

It will be so horrible.

It will be so great!

I reached for the brake cord and prepared to snap it off.

Should I? I thought wickedly.

The face in the ring nodded.

Go for it, Beth. Do it! DO IT!

My fingers began to tingle. They felt cold.

The cold feeling rose up my arm. It spread through my whole body.

Oh, no, I thought. It's happening again.

I'm going out of control.

My fingers touched the brake cord.

The evil welled up in me. I tried to press it back down.

No! I screamed at myself. Don't let it take over!

My fingers wrapped around the cord.

Come on, a voice in my head said. *It will be so easy. And so much fun!*

No! I thought. No!

What am I doing?

I shook my head hard. Snap out of it! I thought.

I don't want to do this! The *ring* wants me to!

I snatched my hand away from the bike. No! I won't do it!

I can't let this happen!

The ring began to burn on my finger. I refused to look at the face.

I've got to get out of here, I realized. I can't resist the power of the ring!

I jumped on my bike and began pedaling frantically.

"Beth — wait!" I heard Danny call. "Where are you going?"

I didn't answer. I didn't even look back.

I knew I had to get away from there.

I've got to get rid of this ring, I thought.

I pedaled furiously toward home. A strong wind seemed to come from nowhere. It blew against me, pushing me back.

I struggled to bike against the wind. My bike barely moved. My legs felt heavy.

It's the evil, I realized. It's trying to stop me!

"No!" I cried. "I won't let you control me!"

The powerful force pushed me back. I could barely breathe in the powerful rush of wind. It was trying to make me hurt all those kids!

I shut my eyes and pumped my legs as hard as I could. I won't! I vowed. I won't give up!

I kept pedaling, using all my strength.

At last, exhausted, I rolled into my driveway. I let my bike drop onto the grass and hurried inside.

I ran straight to the basement. This ring is coming off now! I declared.

I tore over to Dad's workbench. I stopped.

Chirpy's cage sat on a table next to the bench.

Chirpy lay inside the cage. His eyes were closed.

I tapped on the cage. "Chirpy? Chirpy?"

He didn't move.

Chirpy was dead.

Mom must have brought him down here so I wouldn't find him when I got home, I realized. She wanted to tell me about it first.

Poor little bird, I thought sadly. I tried my best to save him.

Then I felt the ring burning on my finger again.

No time to worry about Chirpy now, I thought. I can't think of anything else — not until this ring is off.

I opened Dad's toolbox and shuffled through his tools. Pliers, screwdrivers . . . aha! Metal cutters!

Just what I need, I thought. This ought to do the trick.

I grabbed the metal cutters and raised them to the ring.

"I'll cut you off," I growled at the face.

The tip of the cutters touched the ring.

Suddenly, the ring began to glow.

It warmed on my finger.

"No!" I warned. "You can't stop me!"

I gripped the ring with the metal cutters. The

ring glowed even more brightly. The shiny black jewel began to feel hot.

Black smoke poured out of the ring. Thick, choking smoke. Waves of smoke.

I couldn't help it. I dropped the metal cutters.

I coughed and began to choke as smoke filled the room.

Can't breathe . . . can't breathe . . .

I raised the ring to my face. "Stop it!" I pleaded. "Stop!"

The smoke filled my throat. Tears stung my eyes.

"I can't see!" I choked out. "Can't breathe!"

The ring scalded my hand.

And then the face floated up. Floated out of the ring.

Just a smoky, shifting, ghostly form. The smoke surrounded a gaunt face. The face in the ring, now huge. Empty eyes, a nose, and an evil mouth. All made out of smoke.

The face rose over me. And opened its mouth wide.

Wider. Wider.

As if to swallow me whole.

I shrank back against the workbench, my heart thudding in my chest.

My eyes burned as I stared through the swirling smoke, stared up in horror at the floating face.

"My evil has outgrown the ring!" he bellowed. "Now I need a living body to survive. Now I will possess you!"

"No!" I shrieked. "Please —"

"You can't escape," the face warned. "No one can!"

Through the choking smoke, I eyed the basement steps.

Could I make a run for it?

The creature seemed to read my mind. "Don't try to run away," he rasped. "I will possess you as I possessed your teacher."

"Miss Gold!" I gasped. Once again, I remembered how strange she'd looked at the carnival. How powerful and evil she was.

"When the police captured your teacher, I slipped off her finger," the creature explained. "She was no use to me anymore. Now I have prepared you. The things you have done until now were only little tests. You thought they were evil. To me they were nothing!"

He laughed again, a horrible, raspy laugh.

My body shuddered, gripped in terror.

"Now you are ready, Beth," he said. "Ready for me to leave the ring once again. I will live inside you. Together we can do some REAL evil!"

"No!" I protested. "I won't let you! I'll fight you! I'll fight you the whole way!"

"You have no choice," the face roared. "You wear the ring. And now, I will wear *you*!"

"No . . . no . . ." I begged

"I must have life!" the creature boomed.

The black mist floated down on me. So cold. So cold.

The face hovered, closer, closer . . .

The ring, I thought. I've got to get it off!

I stared wildly through the smoke. Something flashed. Something metal, lying on the workbench.

A saw.

That's it, I thought. I have no choice.

There's only one way to get rid of the ring.

I have to cut off my finger.

I reached for the saw as the black mist surrounded me. Colder, colder . . .

I gripped the wooden handle. I took a deep breath.

I held the saw to my ring finger — and prepared to cut it off.

26

I gulped and held my breath.

My hand shook as I pressed the saw against my finger.

The black smoke swirled around me. I tried not to breathe it in.

The face pressed toward mine.

So cold . . . so cold . . .

My body was filling up with cold.

You have to do it! I told myself. Before the evil takes you over!

Then I saw the dead bird, lying on its side. Wait a minute, I thought.

Maybe there's another way.

The bird . . .

I dropped the saw. It clattered to the floor.

I tugged at the ring with all my might. The ring felt lighter with the face no longer inside.

Come off, I begged. Come off!

WHOOSH!

To my shock, the ring slipped off my finger.

Yes! I thought.

I reached for Chirpy and jammed the ring on his foot.

Above me, the face contorted into a horrible scowl. "NOOOOO!" he screeched. "Nooooooooo!"

The face rose up toward the ceiling. The cold melted out of my body. I rubbed my hands together. I began to warm up.

The smoke hung in the air. I could see the evil face in the swirling mist, fighting to keep away from the bird.

Then, with a final scream, the smoky face was sucked into the body of the dead bird.

It was as if I'd turned on a fan and blown it all away.

I took a deep breath in the clear air. I watched Chirpy closely.

Did it work? I wondered. Did I get rid of him?

Chirpy's body stirred slightly. Oh, no, I thought. I hope the evil won't come alive inside Chirpy!

But Chirpy only shuddered once. Then he gave a choking gasp and fell still.

I poked the bird. Dead.

I began to tremble all over. I can't believe it, I thought.

Did I really kill the evil spirit?

There's only one way to find out, I realized.

Very carefully, I reached into the cage and plucked out the black ring.

I gazed into the jewel.

"Yes!" I cried.

The ring was perfectly clear. No smoky face inside the jewel.

It sparkled and shone like a black diamond.

The evil needed life, I realized. But I gave him death.

And it killed him. It worked!

I started to giggle. Soon I was laughing with joy.

"I did it! I did it!" I shouted. "I killed the evil spirit! I freed myself!"

I danced around the basement, whooping with happiness.

"I got rid of the evil!" I sang. "I did it myself! Yes! Yes! Yes!"

I paused, panting. Still, I thought, I'd better make sure.

I decided to bury Chirpy and the ring in a deep hole. Then I'd never have to worry about evil again.

I found a small wooden box. I placed poor Chirpy's stiff body inside.

"Good-bye, Chirpy," I said. "I'm sorry I couldn't save you. But thanks for saving *me*."

I set the black ring beside him. Then I nailed the box shut.

I grabbed a shovel and took the little casket outside behind the garage. I started to dig. I dug as deep a hole as I could.

I set the box in the hole and covered it with dirt. Then I marked the grave with a stick.

I'd better tell Mom that Chirpy is buried there, I thought. That way she won't dig it up to plant flowers or something.

Wiping the dirt from my hands, I hummed as I headed inside. Mom and Amanda were gone, I realized. They'd been gone the whole time.

They must be out shopping, I thought.

I remembered all the mean things I'd done to Amanda that week. I felt sorry about it. From now on I'm going to be extra-nice to her, I promised myself.

I heard a car door slam. Amanda raced into the house. Mom followed.

"Beth!" Amanda cried. "Beth — look! Look what Mom bought me!"

I smiled and asked, "What is it?"

Amanda held her hands behind her back. She was hiding whatever it was from me. She wanted to surprise me.

That's so cute, I thought.

"Mom knew I was upset about my Barbies being ruined," Amanda explained. "So she bought me a present!"

She held out one hand. "Look! It's a black ring — just like yours!"

I gasped. Amanda held the ring up to show me. The black jewel flashed.

Amanda narrowed her eyes at me. Her face took on a strange, cold glow.

"It even has a face inside!" she cried. "Isn't that cool?"

About R.L. Stine

R.L. Stine is the most popular author in America. He is the creator of the *Goosebumps, Give Yourself Goosebumps, Fear Street*, and *Ghosts of Fear Street* series, among other popular books. He has written over 250 scary novels for kids. Bob lives in New York City with his wife, Jane, teenage son, Matt, and dog, Nadine.

Welcome to the new millennium of fear

Check out this
chilling preview of
what's next from
R.L. STINE

Return to
Ghost Camp

4

"Hey, this place is pretty cool." The guys lowered me from their shoulders. I glanced around the cabin.

It had two bunk beds. Two small dressers. And a poster of Mark McGwire hanging on one wall. A dartboard hung on another wall.

"Where is the counselor's bunk?" I asked.

"Apache cabin doesn't get a counselor," Noah said. "I told you — Apache cabin is the best!"

"I feel sorry for your friend Dustin." Jason shook his head. "The mosquitoes in that cabin will eat him alive."

"The mosquitoes aren't so bad," Noah disagreed. "The bedbugs are worse."

Mosquitoes? Bedbugs? Ari probably hates me by now, I thought. But this identity switch was his idea. Not mine, I told myself, trying not to feel guilty. He wanted to be me — Dustin.

"Ari, give me your duffel. I'll help you unpack." Ben grabbed my duffel and started emptying it.

"You get the two top drawers," Noah said. "Only the best for you, Ari."

I watched in disbelief as he took my T-shirts and shorts from Ben and placed them neatly in the drawers.

What's *with* these guys? I wondered again. Are they this nice to everyone?

While Ben and Noah put my stuff away, I studied the bunks. The two top ones were really great. And one had a small window over it.

One of the bottom beds wasn't too bad, either. But the other was in the darkest corner of the cabin.

That one will probably be mine, I thought. I'm the new kid here, so I'll get the worst bed.

I didn't mind, though. How could I — with everyone being so nice to me?

I sat down on the dark bed.

"Hey — you can't sleep there!" Jason protested.

"Sorry." I jumped up.

"That's your bed." Jason pointed to the top bunk with the window. The best one in the cabin.

"Are — are you sure?" I stammered.

"Sure, we're sure," Ben said. "You the man!"

Ben and Noah stopped unpacking and everyone gave me high fives again.

"Hey, Ari. Catch!"

I turned around and caught a candy bar Jason tossed to me. As I unwrapped it, he guided me over to a big trunk.

"Look inside," he said.

I opened the lid and peered in. "Whoa!" The trunk was filled to the top with candy bars, soda, chips, and cookies.

"It's all for you." Jason grinned.

"Huh? For me?" I repeated, amazed.

"Yep." Jason plunged his hands deep into the trunk. He shoved fistfuls of candy at me. "You the man! Anything you want — just tell us."

"Anything," Ben repeated. "You just tell us."

"We can't believe how lucky we got. We can't believe you're in our cabin." Noah pumped a fist in the air.

"Why? What's going on, guys?" I asked.

The cabin fell silent.

The smiles faded from their faces.

No one moved. No one said a word. They stood there, staring at me strangely.

Jason lowered his eyes to the floor.

Ben folded his arms across his chest.

The room was so silent, I could hear my wrist-watch ticking.

I shoved my hands into my pockets. I shifted my weight from one foot to the other, waiting for someone to say something.

Finally, Noah spoke. "You know why you're

here, right?" he said quietly. "You know what you have to do? Right, Ari?"

I stared back at them.

My heart pounded in my chest.

"Uh . . . right," I said.

"Okay!" Ben unfolded his arms.

Jason tossed me a can of soda.

Everyone started unpacking their stuff. Telling jokes. Eating candy.

I climbed up on my bunk bed and watched them silently.

What do they mean? I wondered.

What do I have to do?

5

"So — where are we going?" I asked Noah that night.

"Just follow us," he said.

Noah, Ben, and Jason led me out of the cabin. I glanced at the cabins around the lake. At the trees edging the woods. All black shadows now.

"Let's go back to the cabin," I said. "I'll get my flashlight."

"We don't need a flashlight," Ben said. "We know where we're going."

"Um — where *are* we going?" I asked again, trying not to sound frightened.

"You'll see." Jason walked behind me. He gave me a shove from behind. "Keep walking."

We circled the lake. I heard the loud drone of insects. It was too dark to see them. But they seemed to be everywhere. Flitting in the tree branches above me. Nesting in the grass at my feet.

I heard croaking. Chirping. Buzzing.

I swatted a mosquito that buzzed in my ear.

Where are they taking me? My heart began to race.

Noah marched us across the front of the mess hall.

As we rounded the corner of the long cobblestone building, an orange glow lit up the night sky.

"Oh, a campfire." I let out a sigh of relief.

"It's a Camp Full Moon tradition," Ben said. "We always have a campfire the first night of camp."

The campfire blazed in the middle of a circle of stones. The whole camp was there — all the campers and all the counselors. Even Uncle Lou.

Kids stood around the fire. Or sat cross-legged in the grass. Eating hot dogs and chugging down fruit punch.

Off to the side, a long picnic table was piled high with a mountain of food.

"Sit right there." Noah pointed to a big boulder on the ground. "We'll get you something to eat."

I didn't want to sit by myself. I glanced around for Ari, but I couldn't find him in the crowd of campers.

"I'll go with you," I said. I jumped up and headed for the food table.

"No way," Jason declared. "We'll bring you plenty of stuff to eat. Relax."

The guys returned with hot dogs, juice, and fries. Before I finished my first hot dog, Noah jumped up and got me another one.

They stared at me as I ate.

"Everything okay?" Ben asked. "Do you need more mustard?"

"No, thanks," I said.

"Did I put *too much* mustard on your hot dog?" Noah jumped up again. "I'll wipe it off for you."

"Everything's great. Really," I said.

I bit into my second hot dog — and a giant bee landed on it.

I almost let out a shriek.

But the guys were staring at me.

I stifled my scream. I tried to slow my pounding heart.

I'm Ari now, I reminded myself. I'm a different person. I'm *not* afraid of bees.

I took a deep breath — then brushed the bee away.

But another bee began circling us. Then another.

Then dozens of them.

It was as if someone had upset a hive — and now the bees were upset with us! They dove at the food. Circled the open juice bottles. Settled in the fries.

They buzzed around my head.

It was my worst nightmare. I wanted to run.

I'm Ari now. I stared down at two bees buzzing around my hot dog. I'm not afraid of bees. I'm not afraid —

"ARI!" The real Ari called out to me. As he walked up to us, he scratched his arms. Then his legs. Then his arms again.

"Dustin! I've been looking for you!" I said. I dropped the hot dog and leaped to my feet.

"We'll be right back." Noah stood. "We're going to get you more juice."

"And marshmallows," Jason added. "I'll toast them for you. How do you like them? Black and crispy — or warm and gooey?

"Uh — crispy," I said.

"He's toasting your marshmallows?" Ari asked in disbelief. He pulled me aside. "Look, Dustin. I don't think this is working. I want to switch back." He scratched his cheek.

"Can't we do it just a little longer?"

He shook his head no. "This isn't fair. My cabin is the pits. There's a hole in the roof. The floor stinks from rot. And the mattresses are crawling with fleas." He scratched his head.

Ugh. Fleas. I took a step away from him.

"I know it's not fair. We'll switch back. In a few

days. I'm having so much fun being you. Please," I begged. "Just a few more days."

"Give me a break," Ari said, bending down to scratch his ankles. "I think my fleas have fleas."

"Please. Just a few more days," I pleaded.

Ari let out a sigh. "Okay. But just a few more days."

He glanced over at the food table, where Noah, Ben, and Jason were piling my plate high with food.

"I should be the one getting the special treatment — not you," he complained.

"Why do they like you so much?" I glanced over at the guys.

Ari shrugged. "I don't have a clue."

"Hey, Dustin," one of Ari's bunk mates called out to him. "I'm ready."

"That's Melvin." Ari groaned. "I have to go. He wants to show me his shoelace collection."

Ari shuffled away, scratching the back of his neck.

I sat down on the ground, waiting for the guys to return.

I glanced at a kid I didn't know. He sat a few feet away from me, stuffing a handful of fries into his mouth.

Two bees landed on his plate.

He stared down at them.

A slow smile spread across his face.

Then, with one swift move, he scooped the bees up in the palm of his hand.

He lifted his hand to his ear. Listened to the trapped bees buzz wildly.

Then he brought his hand to his lips.

He popped the bees into his mouth — and swallowed.

Did I really see that? I blinked hard. Did that kid really swallow two bees?

I shook my head. No. He didn't swallow bees, I told myself. Nobody swallows bees. It had to be a hot dog. Two small chunks of hot dog.

"Yo! Mooners! Gather round!" Uncle Lou stood in front of the campfire. "You know what they say: Time waits for no one! So — let's get started."

Start what? I wondered.

I sat in front of the circle of stones and stared into the fire. I watched the orange-and-yellow flames lick the air. I listened to the sharp crackle of the firewood as it burned.

I took a deep breath, breathing in the fire's woody smell.

Maybe sleep-away camp isn't going to be so bad, I thought. As long as I can be Ari.

"Okay! It's time for our traditional Full Moon welcome!" Uncle Lou announced.

He tugged his shorts up over his big belly. Then he lifted a whistle to his lips and gave a long, loud blow.

All the campers stood up. They threw back their heads and howled at the moon. Then they cheered: "Old Mooners. Full Mooners. Let's hear it for the NEW MOONERS!" Then they all howled again.

Ari sat down behind me. "This is a really friendly camp," he leaned forward and whispered in my ear. "I thought new campers were supposed to be treated like dirt."

"And a very special welcome for Ari Davis!" Uncle Lou pumped a fist in the air.

Huh?

"Ari. Ari. Ari," the whole camp chanted.

My cheeks grew hot.

"Ari. Ari. Ari," they cheered, stamping their feet, piercing the night with sharp howls.

"Apache cabin rules!" Noah shouted.

What is it with everyone around here? I wondered.

"They should be cheering for *me*." Ari leaned forward again. "This isn't fair," he whispered bitterly.

"We'll switch back soon," I promised.

A tall, skinny counselor carried a bench over to the fire. He had a buzz cut and a big space between his two front teeth. He set the bench down next to Uncle Lou.

"Nate, one of us has to lose sixty pounds," Uncle Lou joked. Then he lowered himself onto the bench.

"I think Uncle Lou is getting ready to tell us the story," Ben said.

The campers grew quiet.

"What story?" I asked.

But I didn't listen to the answer. I heard a rustling sound from the woods.

I turned and gazed into the dark trees that surrounded the campfire.

Something was out there.

I saw a pair of red glowing eyes. Animal eyes shining through the trees.

Then I saw a flash. Another pair of glowing eyes. Then another flash.

Dozens of red glowing eyes. Flickering in the woods. Staring at us.

A shiver ran down my spine as I watched the dark woods flicker with the eerie light.

What's out there? I wondered.

Whatever they are, I realized, they've got us completely surrounded!

"**T**his is the legend of The Snatcher,"
Uncle Lou began.

Everyone grew silent.

The campfire crackled behind Uncle Lou.

His voice was low. But I could hear him perfectly.

The campers sat totally still. Leaning forward
slightly. Listening closely.

My eyes darted to the woods. To the glowing animal eyes flickering among the trees.

I wanted to ask one of the guys about them. Ask
if they knew what was out there. But Noah, Ben,
and Jason were leaning forward too, concentrating on Uncle Lou.

I turned away from the flashing red eyes.

I tried to forget that they were out there watching — staring at us.

"When the full moon rises — that's when he comes." Uncle Lou's voice grew lower.

"Who comes?" I whispered to Noah. "Did I miss something?"

"Shhhh." Noah placed his fingers to his lips. "Listen. Listen carefully, Ari."

"Come back with me." Uncle Lou closed his eyes. "Travel back twenty-five years — to a sunny day in July. Opening day of a brand-new camp.

"'A camp that should never have been built,' the local people said. They knew the danger. But no one would listen to them.

"Campers arrived all day long. They unpacked their bags and trunks. Laughing. Talking about the big campfire planned for that night. A big grand-opening celebration.

"And it was a big day for Johnny Grant. His first day at sleep-away camp.

"'Have fun!' Johnny's father ruffled his son's curly brown hair. 'See you in August!'

"Johnny's mother kissed him good-bye.

"She didn't know what was about to happen. How could she? Nobody knew."

"What didn't they know?" I heard Ari ask someone.

Someone shushed him.

"Finally the sun set," Uncle Lou continued. "It was a warm summer evening. A full moon hung in the sky. The lake seemed to glow under its soft, shimmering golden light."

As Uncle Lou spoke, I glanced over at the lake — and gasped. The lake was glowing! I gazed up into the sky — at the full moon that hung there.

This is just a story, I told myself. But I couldn't help it — I started to shiver.

"A campfire burned," Uncle Lou went on. "Campers gathered around it. Toasting marshmallows. So excited to be there. So excited to be the first campers at a brand-new camp — Camp Full Moon."

A soft murmur ran through our campsite. Uncle Lou waited for everyone to quiet down. Then he continued.

"After everyone ate and the fire died down, the counselors set out lanterns. The campers sat among the glowing lights. As they sang camp songs, a pack of red foxes gathered in the woods.

"They quietly made their way to the forest's edge. So quietly — no one heard them.

"They stared out from the trees. Stared out at the campers."

I thought about the flashing eyes in the woods. But I was too scared to see if they were still there. I kept my eyes on Uncle Lou.

Uncle Lou took a deep breath.

"Johnny Grant wandered away from the campfire. So happy to be at camp. So eager to explore. He headed for the trees.

"A few kids saw him leave. But no one called out to him. No one stopped him.

"Suddenly, a cry rang out from the trees. A voice screaming, 'Help me!' A tortured scream. A scream of pain.

"Everyone ran into the woods.

"They saw the foxes.

"But one of the foxes wasn't really a fox.

"It was The Snatcher.

"The local people knew all about The Snatcher. An evil creature that took the form of a fox. It hid among them and prowled the woods. Searching for its next victim.

"And now Johnny knew about The Snatcher too. His first day of camp — was his last. He was never seen again.

"Beware of The Snatcher," Uncle Lou whispered. "It can take any form. And it's watching. Always watching."

Uncle Lou opened his eyes. "Okay. Story's over."

I gazed around the campfire at the campers. At their terrified faces.

Why do they look *so* frightened?

I was scared too. But ghost stories are supposed to be scary. Aren't they?

"That was a good one," I heard one of the new campers say. "Uncle Lou tells great horror stories."

"The story is true," one of the counselors warned. "You'd better be careful. One kid vanishes every year from this camp. Taken away by The Snatcher — and never seen again!"

"Yeah, right." The camper laughed. "Look at me. I'm shaking."

The campers slowly drifted away from the campfire.

Drifted back to their bunks.

I stared into the campfire. Watched the embers flicker and die.

When I started to turn away from the fire, someone grabbed me from behind.

I tried to scream — but a hand clamped down hard on my mouth.

I kicked and twisted — but I couldn't break free.

The hands gripped me tightly.

And roughly dragged me back into the woods.

"Let me go!" I struggled to cry out. But the hand over my mouth pressed harder. Pressed my lips hard against my teeth.

I kicked. I twisted.

But I wasn't strong enough.

I was dragged deeper into the woods.

Out of sight of the glowing campfire.

"Okay. Let him go," a voice whispered.

The hands fell away.

I whirled around — and stared into Jason's eyes. Ben and Noah stood beside him.

"Sorry, Ari. Hope I didn't hurt you," Jason apologized.

I realized that my legs were trembling.

"Why did you drag me out here?" I shouted, trying to hide my fear.

"We want to talk to you," Noah said. "We have to make sure no one hears us." Noah's eyes darted from tree to tree.

"What's so important?" I asked.

He took a step toward me. "We have to talk to you about The Snatcher."

Huh?

"That dumb story?" I said.

"Why are you saying that?" Ben asked.

"Because that's what it is — just a dumb camp story," I replied.

"Oh, I get it." Jason smiled at me. "You're kidding around with us."

"Are you, Ari? Are you kidding around?" Ben demanded.

I didn't answer. I stared down at my feet. I kicked a rock in the dirt.

"You told us you understood." Noah stepped toward me. "In the cabin this afternoon — you told us you knew what you had to do." Noah's eyes narrowed. The muscles in his face tightened.

"Stop being so hard on him." Jason tried to calm Noah down. "Ari knows. Right?"

"Do you know?" Noah took another step toward me.

What are they talking about? My head began to throb. *What should I say?*

I backed away. Backed hard into a tree trunk.

The boys moved forward.

Started to close in on me.

What do they want? My heart began to pound.

I quickly glanced around.

The woods were dark.

We were totally alone out here.

They stepped closer.

If I scream, will anyone hear me?

"You the man, Ari," Ben said. "You're the one!"

They stepped closer — and I ran.

I darted through the trees, heading for the cabins.

I ran as fast as I could — searching for the clearing. Searching for the lake. Searching for the mess hall.

But I couldn't find any sign of camp.

I stopped. Spun around.

Nothing but trees.

Where is the camp?

Did I get turned around?

Where should I run?

The woods were filled with mosquitoes. They swarmed around my face. Flew into my eyes. Sunk their stingers into my neck, my cheeks.

I started to run again.

Mouth open. Panting hard.

Swatting mosquitoes.

I ran into a cloud of gnats. They flew into my mouth. My ears.

I shook my head wildly.

I ran and ran.

A sharp pain stabbed my side.

I stopped. Gulped air. Rubbed the pain in my ribs.

Heard the snap of a twig behind me — and froze.

I slowly turned around — and stared into the eyes of a fox.

A red fox.

Panting hungrily.

Staring back at me with glowing eyes.

 stumbled back.

I kept my eyes on the fox.

The Snatcher.

The words floated into my mind.

Just a silly story, I told myself. Just a silly camp story.

Another pair of glowing eyes moved among the trees.

Then another.

All around me, the woods shimmered in red light.

The eerie light grew brighter as the foxes closed in.

My chest tightened.

I stared into a bright pair of eyes. Brighter than all the rest. Red-hot, intense as laser light.

Are those the eyes of The Snatcher?

Another pair of eyes loomed close by.

Or are those?

My heart raced. My clothes were drenched with sweat.

There were glowing red eyes everywhere I turned.

Just a story, I repeated. Just a story . . .

I spun away. Tried to run.

But I froze at the sound of an angry snarl.

And cried out in horror as a fox leaped into the air . . .

PREPARE TO BE SCARED!

Goosebumps
SERIES 2000
R.L. STINE

☐	BCY39988-8	#1: Cry of the Cat
☐	BCY39990-X	#2: Bride of the Living Dummy
☐	BCY39989-6	#3: Creature Teacher
☐	BCY39991-8	#4: Invasion of the Body Squeezers (Part I)
☐	BCY39992-6	#5: Invasion of the Body Squeezers (Part II)
☐	BCY39993-4	#6: I Am Your Evil Twin
☐	BCY39994-2	#7: Revenge R Us
☐	BCY39995-0	#8: Fright Camp
☐	BCY39996-9	#9: Are You Terrified Yet?
☐	BCY76781-X	#10: Headless Halloween
☐	BCY76783-6	#11: Attack of the Graveyard Ghouls
☐	BCY76784-4	#12: Brain Juice
☐	BCY18733-3	#13: Return to HorrorLand
☐	BCY68517-1	#14: Jekyll and Heidi
☐	BCY68519-8	#15: Scream School
☐	BCY68520-1	#16: The Mummy Walks
☐	BCY68521-X	#17: The Werewolf in the Living Room

$3.99 Each!